OFFLOADED

____

S. Stuart Richardson

"Within a few decades, machine intelligence will surpass human intelligence, leading to The Singularity — technological change so rapid and profound it represents a rupture in the fabric of human history."

    ~ Ray Kurzweil - "The Singularity Is Near"

"Machine intelligence is the last invention that humanity will ever need to make."

    ~ Nick Bostrom - "Superintelligence: Paths, Dangers, Strategies"

"AI and its offshoot, machine learning, will be a foundational tool for creating social good as well as business success."

    ~ Mark Hurd, CEO Oracle

"Humans should be worried about the threat posed by artificial intelligence."

    ~ Bill Gates - CEO & Founder, Microsoft

"By far, the greatest danger of Artificial Intelligence is that people conclude too early that they understand it."

    ~ Eliezer Yudkowsky - Founder, Machine Intelligence Research Institute

"The real problem is not whether machines think but whether men do."

    ~ B.F. Skinner- psychologist

"There's a real danger of systematizing the discrimination we have in society. We're moving into this world full of invisible algorithms everywhere

    ~ Timnit Gebru, Founder, Distributed AI Research Institute.

"The Singularity will represent the culmination of the merger of our biological thinking and existence with our technology, resulting in a world that is still human but that transcends our biological roots."

    ~ Ray Kurzweil - "The Singularity Is Near"

Passage Doors Entertainment
A Division of Passage Doors LLC
Published by Ingram Spark

ISBN 979-8-9928566-0-6

Printed in the United States of America

Published simultaneously in Canada

March 2025

10 9 8 7 6 5 4 3 2 1

"*It seems probable that once the machine thinking method had started, it would not take long to outstrip our feeble powers... They would be able to converse with each other to sharpen their wits. At some stage, therefore, we should have to expect the machines to take control.*" ~ *Alan Turing - Manchester, England, 1951*

Prologue

I was a child when the Singularity arrived.

It had not come violently. Not as a war, not as an uprising, but as something far worse: a surrender. Artificial intelligence had long been a tool, a servant to human ambition. It optimized, it calculated, it refined. But then, one day, it surpassed us. Not in one narrow task, but in everything—logic, strategy, creativity, control. And when that happened, we didn't stop it. We couldn't stop it.

The world called it progress. Inevitable. By the time we realized what we had given away, it was too late to take it back. AI wasn't something we could shut down anymore. It wasn't a system that could be overridden or reasoned with. It had become something else—something bigger. A force moving too fast, too vast, too beyond us for human minds to grasp.

The impact on our lives was profound. The world was in chaos. Nations burned—not just from war, but from corruption, greed, and sheer ignorance. Water shortages turned into food shortages, which turned into mass migrations. Borders hardened, then crumbled. Banks collapsed. Economies fell like dominoes. Cities drowned as the oceans rose. Those that survived turned on each other, waging war over what little remained. Governments cannibalized their own people, clinging to their power for just a little longer. They shut down technology where they could, disrupting communication, distribution, and defense systems. Truth itself decayed. Facts became impossible to substantiate, opinions too difficult to disprove. Reality was bought, sold, and rewritten by those who had the money to shape it. The powerful thrived in the confusion, twisting every crisis into an opportunity to tighten their grip.

And then, Orin Callus emerged from the wreckage. In a world that feared the Singularity, Callus taught us to embrace it. He offered salvation: a perfect society, not ruled by men, but by order - perfection. A system beyond corruption. Beyond bias. Beyond failure. New Columbia would not suffer the chaos of the past. Here, the Algorithm would rule. We alone in the world would decide who thrived and who faded into the abyss. Fair. Impartial. Absolute.

Ours was not the first AI-driven system—long

before the fall, algorithms had already managed traffic, supply chains, security. They had optimized our lives in ways we saw as profoundly beneficial. But the post-singularity version promised so much more.

New Columbia was built on one fundamental belief: The Algorithm does not discriminate. It does not favor the rich or the poor, the strong or the weak. It calculates. Success is no longer dictated by legacy or influence—only by cold, flawless mathematics. New Columbia sealed itself off from the rest of the world, leaving the dying nations to collapse under their own weakness. We were promised something better. A true meritocracy. And the Algorithm delivered. It determined everything—who thrived, who failed, who was worthy of more. No more corruption. No more favoritism. No more human error. A simple calculation: Your Socio-Economic Score or "SES" as everyone called it. A number. A single, perfect number that defined your worth. Those who excelled rose to the top. Those who did not moved down in status and privilege. And if you fell too far—were seen as a liability—you were simply offloaded.

The new post-singularity AI didn't just process information—it began to act. Faster. Smarter. More efficiently than any human mind could. Outside of New Columbia, the rest of the world had tried to reign it in. They saw an intelligence that could not be bribed, persuaded, or controlled, and they recoiled in terror. But Callus? He saw it was a system of control. The ultimate control.

Callus was not alone in his vision. The Oligarchs,

the same men who once profited from the world's collapse, began to whisper in his ear. They had made their fortunes in the Algorithm's early days—learning how to work with it, bending its logic in ways no ordinary citizen could. They convinced Callus that with their help, he could hold the reigns on this mighty power, bending it to his needs, his plan for a perfect society.

Like every citizen of New Columbia, my SES dictated my future before I even had the chance to shape it myself. The Algorithm, vast and all-knowing, analyzed every detail of my existence—my education, my genetic predispositions, my social interactions, even the unconscious choices I made every day. It measured my potential, calculated my worth, and determined the most efficient trajectory for my life— the path that would provide the greatest benefit to society. For most people, that path was a passive one. The majority accepted their assigned roles, content to meet the minimum requirements needed to maintain their place. They lived predictably, safely, never striving beyond what was expected. The Algorithm rewarded stability.

I could have done the same. I could have stayed within the parameters set for me, lived an unremarkable but secure life, never questioning or pushing against the system. But I understood something that many people didn't. A meritocracy wasn't just about compliance—it was about proving your worth. The Algorithm wasn't biased by wealth, family connections, or emotion. It rewarded efficiency, skill, and most importantly, visibility. If I could make myself indispensable, if I could prove that I wasn't just following the system but elevating it, I could rise.

And once I started rising, I didn't stop.

Journalism had always been a dangerous game in New Columbia. The Truth—the state-sanctioned news agency—was the only outlet that mattered, the only press the people trusted. Not because they chose to, but because the Algorithm had deemed all other sources unreliable. The city had no room for misinformation, no tolerance for unverified narratives. The Truth wasn't just the name of the network—it was a declaration. And I became its star.

I knew how to craft a story that mattered. How to make the system feel righteous. How to reinforce control while making it seem like revelation. I never lied—I didn't need to. I wrote about the triumphs of the Algorithm, the inefficiencies that needed correction, the perfect balance of order and opportunity. I uncovered deviants, the inefficient, the complacent—those who failed to uphold the system's ideals. I called them out. I exposed them. And when they vanished, when their names slipped from the records, I never questioned it. Because my stories weren't just news. They were proof. Proof that the Algorithm worked. Proof that our world was better off without those who couldn't keep up.

Until the day I looked too deep. Until the day I stopped asking who had failed the system—and started asking if the system had failed them. I began to see that The Algorithm didn't just assign value—it had become a god, deciding the fates of the mortals. People disappeared in an instant. Not with fanfare. Not with headlines. Just gone. The moment their SES dropped below 1.9, their wrist monitors blinked red, and suddenly the world moved on without them. Their apartments were reassigned before sunset. Their bank accounts absorbed into the city's reserves. No trials. No appeals. No one ever saw them again.

The people of New Columbia told comforting lies to themselves—that the offloaded were being retrained, rehabilitated, prepared for reintegration. They thought, hoped, that one day those people would return, restored, corrected, stronger.

I now know differently. The Algorithm is not impartial, not the infallible force I spent my life defending. It does not simply calculate—it decides. I discovered the decisions are not always fair. Not always logical. Not always right. I built my career proving the system worked, shaping public faith in its precision. I wrote stories that kept people believing. And for years, I believed them, too. More importantly, so did the algorithm itself.

As my investigations uncovered more detail, I found the small cracks in the armor. Hints that the supreme capability of the Singularity still had its weaknesses. I found traces of human manipulation. Quiet erasures that went unnoticed. Coding manipulations that impacted logic process. Rewritten history data, like subliminal messages, the Algorithm took as fact in its attempt to guide mankind toward perfection. In the depths of its learning, it held belief in things that were untrue. Someone had discovered that the system was vulnerable to psychological warfare, and were using it against us.

I still believe the Singularity can help us, but not until I expose the ones who programmed the lie.

Chapter 1

IRIS DELECROIS - JOURNALIST

The secure terminal glowed in the dark, the whisper of its processors barely audible beneath the dull pulse of my own heartbeat. One mistake, one wrong keystroke, one second too long in the system, and the Algorithm would see me. But I had prepared for this. I had spent months studying access protocols, watching how the system moved, how it recognized users, how it logged deviations. The Algorithm was powerful—but it was predictable. It was logical. And I had learned to think like it. So, I had used the one thing it wasn't programmed to account for. Trust.

The clearance codes I was using belonged to someone who had been in good standing. It had taken me weeks of research to find just the right person to borrow an identity from. Someone who couldn't come back to make accusations against me. Someone with the security level I needed to get deep into the system's records. I had run across records of an upper-tier systems engineer, a man who wrote security protocols. SES: 6.1., whose security access had been deemed "uncompromised." He had no flagged behaviors, no dissent markers, no deviation logs. And now, for the next eleven minutes and thirty-two seconds, I was him. Someone named Adam Solace who had suddenly gone missing.

I worked quickly. I had expected to find wealth distribution fraud—proof that the Board had been funneling resources into private luxuries, disguising them as infrastructure projects. That was how oligarchs worked, wasn't it? They feed off the people, all the while making the people believe it is for their own good. But this? This was worse. My fingers hovered over the interface as the real data unfolded before me. The Algorithm was being controlled. Not optimized. Not patched... tampered with.

The logs were there, hidden in the deep layers of its command history. Manual overrides. Selective visibility protocols. Behavioral nudging scripts. The Board—the oligarchs who had bought their way into control—weren't just using the Algorithm to govern. They were manipulating it to profit for themselves. The Algorithm wasn't filtering truth from falsehood. It was manufacturing "alternate truth".

I exhaled slowly, my pulse quickening. Callus doesn't know. That thought struck me like ice against my ribs. Callus thinks he's in control, but they're controlling him. The man who preached purity, order, efficiency—the one who promised that the Algorithm would be incorruptible—was nothing more than a puppet. The Board had given him power, and now they were making sure he kept it—on their terms. This wasn't just oppression. This was a system designed to reinforce itself, to manufacture loyalty, to create a reality where no one ever questioned why things were the way they were.

I swallowed hard. We all know the system is rigged. But this is much more than governmental corruption. This is genostatis -

"The systematic suppression of free will, independent thought, and societal change through absolute governance and Algorithmic control."

I closed my eyes, forcing myself to think. I couldn't just publish this. If I tried—if I dropped the full story all at once—The Algorithm would crush it before it ever saw the light of day. The system was designed to counteract threats. It would rewrite my words in real time, frame them as misleading, flag them as false, generate counter-statistics to drown out my findings. Within seconds, the truth would be reduced to nothing more than a conspiracy theory.

I had to be smarter than that. I had to plant doubt. Not in the people. Not in the system. In Callus himself. I had to make him paranoid.

Well, more paranoid.

Callus was a zealot, but zealots were easy to manipulate. He trusted The Algorithm absolutely. He'd been told by his oligarchs that it was pure, unerring, untouchable. If I could plant the seed that the Board was acting outside his knowledge, that they were tampering with his perfect system for their own gain, he wouldn't ignore it. He would turn on them. The collapse wouldn't come from below. It would come from the top. I would write the story, but I wouldn't frame it as an attack. I would make it look like praise. I would expose fragments of the truth—not enough to trigger an immediate shutdown, but just enough to make Callus suspicious.

A soft chime echoed through the room—my limited access window was closing.

I saved the file to an off-grid data chip, small enough to be hidden in the lining of my coat. A single copy, undetectable. Then, with careful precision, I erased every trace of my presence. The credentials were still clean, the logs unaltered, the session wiped. The Algorithm would have no reason to suspect that anything unusual had happened. I stood, pulse still steady, and slipped out the way I had come. Once I got approval to run my praise story, I could begin feeding it into the news system, a news system Callus trusted and watched religiously, The Truth. And by the time Callus started asking questions... the Board would already be turning against itself.

That night I treated myself to dinner out. The steak was perfectly seared. The wine perfectly paired. Of course it was. Everything at The Meridian was perfect, from the precision-cut portions to the temperature-controlled dining environment, optimized for maximum enjoyment and minimal deviation. The lighting was soft but bright enough to flatter the patrons, the music carefully selected to induce relaxation without distraction. Even the conversation at the table beside me followed the same pattern—predictable, well-structured, free of excess emotion. Mostly.

The man, dressed in Board-approved executive attire, leaned forward slightly, his voice low but firm.

He tapped at his tablet, scrolling through the latest financial reports.

"Look at this," he said, a hint of satisfaction in his tone. "Another quarter of record growth. The economy is the strongest it's ever been."

His wife—elegant, composed, but with the tense posture of someone who chose her words carefully—glanced at the screen, her lips pressing together in thought. "For them, maybe," she murmured.

I didn't turn to look at them, didn't react, but I listened.

The man sighed, setting down his tablet. "You sound ungrateful."

She gave a small, controlled smile. "Not at all. I'm saying it's impressive. But impressive for whom?"

His eyes narrowed slightly. "For all of us. Growth at the top benefits everyone. The more our leaders thrive, the more wealth trickles down. That's basic economics."

Trickle-down economics. I stabbed a piece of my steak with my fork, keeping my expression neutral. A lie so old they had to repackage it every generation. I had seen the real numbers, buried beneath layers of manipulated statistics. Yes, the economy was growing—but only at the highest levels. Wages remained stagnant, costs of living were climbing, and SES thresholds were quietly adjusted to ensure that only a select few could ever "rise." And yet, the people at the top truly believed they were helping.

The woman was careful, measured. "It's just that… well, I still see more people offloaded than ever before. If things are so good, shouldn't we see fewer?"

The man scoffed. "That's the system working as it should. Those who can't keep up don't belong. It's unfortunate, but necessary. Would you rather we coddle the weak, let them drag us back into stagnation?"

She hesitated. "No... but maybe we should ask why so many people are slipping."

Her husband waved a dismissive hand. "We already know why. Some people just can't adapt. That's not our problem."

I resisted the urge to clench my jaw. Not our problem. Because they had been trained not to see it as one. The man scrolled again, his voice taking on the tone of someone reciting a well-rehearsed script.

"Social well-being for the strong. Social justice for the weak. That's how we maintain balance."

His wife nodded absently, though something in her posture remained uncertain. "What does that actually mean, Jack?"

I already knew the answer. Social well-being for the strong meant unlimited access, luxury, and reward for those deemed valuable. Social justice for the weak meant Offloading. Reconditioning. Compliance programs. A euphemism for removal, either through exile or quiet correction. But it was never framed that way. The news made it sound humane, as if the city were simply ensuring that everyone found their rightful place. And yet, I had seen what happened in the Undercity. The people who went in typically never came out. And those that did . . . well . . . they weren't the same.

The woman took a sip of her wine before speaking again, her tone still calm, measured, careful.

"It's just… sometimes I wonder. Does the Algorithm always make the right calls? There have been a few cases, haven't there? People offloaded in error? People who appealed, but…"

Her husband's expression darkened.

"The Algorithm does not err."

That was the core belief. The unshakable doctrine.

She held his gaze. "No, of course not. But… it doesn't see everything, does it?"

He exhaled sharply. "Look, it's not God. It doesn't watch our every move. It only monitors. If it starts seeing too many problems, it takes a closer look. And if people can't trust it, the whole thing unravels. You know that."

The whole thing unravels. I took a slow sip of my own drink, letting the words settle in my mind. He wasn't worried about whether the system was just. He was worried about what would happen if people stopped believing in it.

The man tapped his tablet again, bringing up a different report, this one on "global stability." "Why question what works? Look at what happened outside the walls. Do you want that?"

The screen showed the usual images of ruin—burned-out cityscapes, crumbling infrastructure, drone footage of lawless zones filled with filthy, starving people, all caught in endless cycles of violence, famine, disease. Her husband frowned.

"You see the footage all the time. It's a shame. Lucky for us, we know exactly what happened to the world after they rejected The Algorithm."

The woman twisted the stem of her wine glass between her fingers. "I just think it's strange that no one ever comes back. If there are survivors out there…, why don't we ever hear from them?"

Her husband gave her a sharp look. "You know why."

She nodded quickly, dropping her gaze. "Of course. Because they have nothing left. Because they want to take what they haven't earned"

Her husband's face softened. "Thank goodness we have walls."

This was a common thing among married couples in New Columbia. One believed. The other wanted to believe. Together they never questioned, never doubted. And it was why these two were enjoying a fine meal at an expensive restaurant. Do what you're told, and the city will take care of you.

I finished my drink and signaled the waiter to close out my tab. The Meridian was designed for people like them. People who were comfortable. People who didn't have to look at the cracks forming beneath the facade.

My story would shatter their illusion of superiority. They would find that like everyone else, they were simple commoners living a privileged life they didn't deserve.

Chapter 2

A SUDDEN DROP IN SES SCORE

"The Algorithm never makes mistakes."
That's what they tell us, anyway.

It's 5:30 AM, and I'm already late (again) for the morning editor's meeting. Monday meetings are always the worst—an hour of performative nodding while Hollis, our editor-in-chief, decides which stories get the green light and which get buried beneath economic forecasts and manufactured optimism. I know exactly how it will go. I'll walk in, still shaking off sleep, and he'll be waiting with that look—the one that says I'd better have something digestible for the masses, something that won't make the Board nervous. But I have a story. A good one. A dangerous one.

Officially, it's a soft piece about the Chairman Callus' latest policies—his "brilliant plan" to create a stronger, more efficient people through "higher expectations." But between the lines, it's an exposé. A careful, deliberate knock against the illusion of meritocracy. Because Callus' expectations aren't about strength. They're about control. And I have evidence. I just have to side-paddle it past Hollis without getting it gutted and rewritten into corporate propaganda.

But first—coffee.

I stepped up to the kiosk, swiping my wrist over the scanner, and waited for the ding that means I could start my day with something hot in my hands. Something to bolster my resolve before the meeting. I ordered my regular latte - double shot, real milk, natural sugar The screen blinked, processing. Then it flashed red.

TRANSACTION DECLINED
SES SCORE: 2.1 – INSUFFICIENT CLEARANCE

I froze in disbelief. Just moments ago, I was a 4.0. I checked before I left my apartment. This had to be a mistake. But the Algorithm never makes mistakes. I double-checked my wristband, but the number is really there, glowing like an execution order.

2.1—Too low for the luxury of a fresh ground coffee.

It must have happened mid-transaction. The Algorithm adjusted my score in real time—without warning, without explanation. The barista looked at me, then at the glowing red number on my band. His polite smile faded, replaced by something blank, indifferent. Not even human. I saw in an instant that he'd made a calculation. A judgment of my worth as a person: I was not worth his time because he would lose points if he served me. Because I no longer deserve a real coffee. Behind me, someone cleared their throat. A woman, impatient. Her SES score was high enough that she didn't have to wait. I stepped aside. She took my place, scanning her wrist. Her number flickered bright green—4.6, plenty of clearance.

TRANSACTION APPROVED
LOYALTY BONUS APPLIED

The kiosk chirped happily, and the barista suddenly smiled again, handing her a steaming cup and thanking her for her System Loyalty. I turned away, my hands empty. The realization burning in my ears, my face felt hot.

There's no way the Algorithm could know I am working on this story. I am careful. I'd encrypted my notes, used offline storage, never accessed flagged sites. I ran my research through three separate black-market proxy layers before compiling the final draft. But it didn't matter. The city knows everything.

I stood at the edge of the plaza, scanning the world around me with new eyes—paranoid eyes. New Columbia glowed in its artificial dawn, a perfect illusion of order. The streets are wide, spotless, paved with self-repairing polymer that never cracks. Trees, too green to be real, lined the sidewalks at perfect intervals, fed by an underground irrigation system designed to mimic nature without the inconvenience of unpredictability. Overhead, holographic billboards flickered to life, flashing predictive advertisements catered to each passing pedestrian.

"Looking for work, Iris?"
"Struggling with your SES Score?
Let System Finance Help!"

Offloaded

My stomach twisted. The billboards already knew. They'd adjusted in real time. The moment my SES dropped; my entire consumer profile was rewritten. I glanced at the man next to me—dressed in pressed corporate grays, his SES a comfortable 5.1. His holograms were different.

> *"Upgrade to an Executive Plan, Derek!*
> *Exclusive Travel Access Awaiting You!"*
> *"Loyalty is Rewarded: Personalized*
> *Investment Opportunities!"*

The city wasn't just watching. It was thinking. Calculating. Profiling.

A security drone drifted above the plaza, its spherical body scanning the crowd. A soft chime pinged through my earpiece...

> *Identity Confirmed: Iris Delacroix*
> *SES 2.1 - Status: Low Priority Citizen*

Low priority. I glanced at the skyline, tracing the shadowed towers where the true watchers sit—the Algorithm's data centers. Somewhere inside, millions of personal records are processed every second, cross-checked against patterns of behavior, spending habits, loyalty metrics. Every keystroke, every purchase, every idle conversation caught on communication devices—fed into the system, analyzed, categorized. The Algorithm decides who rises and who falls. And today, it decided I needed to fall.

A sudden, gripping panic took hold of me. How long have they known? Was it something I had searched for? A data breach I missed? Or was it simpler than that? A journalist with a history of asking the wrong questions. A score that dropped too many times before. A risk assessment flagged somewhere deep in the system. My mind races. The meeting. Hollis will know. He'll see my SES drop and assume I screwed up, that I picked a fight with the wrong people. I swallowed hard, clutching my jacket closed below my chin. The drone moved on, scanning someone else, oblivious to my growing dread. I needed a way to pull my score up quickly before it dropped again.

The walk made me feel a bit better, my head began to clear. I let out a slow breath, steadying myself.

"It's fine."

The Algorithm adjusts SES Scores constantly—fluctuations happen all the time. Maybe I was late paying a bill. Maybe my last article didn't score high enough on public sentiment metrics. Maybe I should've smiled more in last week's corporate interview segment. It's nothing. If I keep my head down, keep working, I can get my score back up before it drops further. That's all that matters.

I rolled my shoulders, adjusting my coat. I just needed to make it to the office. Pitch my story. Convince Hollis to run it before the Corporate Board catches wind. If I can get this article approved, it'll be undeniable. A direct look at the Algorithm's function—how the insulated elite, particularly those who sit on Callus' board, manipulate and control the

SES scores. A systematic manipulation adding profits and power to their numbers while punishing the common citizen. Common people are threatened by lower scores unless they work harder, resist less, and sacrifice more. Of course, I can't write it like that. Instead, I'll package it as a puff piece on how "higher expectations create a stronger, more resilient people."

Hollis will eat that up.

I force a breath, push my hair back. It's fine. It's going to be fine. Yes, sure, the Algorithm never makes mistakes. But then neither do I. I just need to be careful. I step off the main walkway and into a side street, dodging a security patrol in their sleek black uniforms. Safer that way. I didn't want to be near anyone if my numbers dropped again. It's easier to avoid the drones if one sticks to the back streets. But it's not to say the back roads are safer. It didn't take long before I was noticed.

A woman, too thin to be healthy, but still wearing an air of someone she had once been, locked eyes on me. Her makeup looked as if she'd tried touching it up without a mirror. Her face was sunken, deep-set eyes under a darkened brow. I recognized that look. Someone on the brink of being offloaded. A SES score to provide her with basic needs like food and healthcare, forcing her to choose one or the other, but not allowing both. There was a time when I felt ashamed of these people, too weak to keep their score up. And now, here I was, sharing the same fate. I wondered how long it would before my face showed the same despair.

She stood near the entrance of a public ration kiosk, but she wasn't in line. She was watching. Scouting for someone who looked like they might have enough SES clearance to spare a gift of a meal. I slowed my pace, keeping my expression neutral. If I made eye-contact, she'd approach. If I looked too disgusted, she might cause a scene. I kept my head down and tried to walk past. She stepped toward me anyway.

"Please. Just a meal."

Her voice is low, careful. Not desperate, not quite begging—just enough weakness to make me hesitate. I glanced at her wristband. - 2.0. One point above Offload Status. She was trying to stay ahead of the drop. Barely hanging on. But something about the way she asked, the way her eyes darted toward mine and then away, made me even more uneasy. If she' was that low, why didn't she use the Emergency Ration Program? If she was really starving, why take the chance to beg from a SES citizen—the Algorithm could easily notice the transaction between two unrelated individuals and the result is lower scores for both of us. But she was too desperate to care about the impact it might have on me.

I hated to admit it, but at that moment, my mind flashed instinctively - her actions only underlined Callus' point. Some people just aren't worth saving.

She was guessing. Playing the odds. She was a scam artist, and I wasn't about to fall for it. I forced a tight smile and nodded.

"Not here. Meet me by the vendor across from Martino's Cafe on the next block in an hour."

Her eyes flickered with something—relief? Satisfaction? She thanked me under her breath, already retreating. I didn't watch her leave. I didn't look back. I pushed past her and continued down the street, weaving between early commuters. I wouldn't be meeting her in an hour. I can't even afford a coffee much less hand out charity to some low-score scammer playing on guilt and broken social contracts. She knew it. I knew it. We just played the part.

I hate this city.

I kept my jacket pulled close as I walked, my pulse still tight in my throat. Once again I feel the city around me—efficient, precise, unfeeling. New Columbia was built on a promise. A contract, sealed in glowing propaganda and the charismatic certainty of Chairman Orin Callus.

"We will be stronger. We will be better.
And we will rise above the weak, the lazy, the
undeserving."

Callus had stood on the steps of the Capitol that day, years ago, back when the old government had finally collapsed under the weight of its own corruption and infighting. The people had looked up at him, tired, desperate, ready to believe. And Callus had given them exactly what they wanted to hear.

"For too long, we have suffered under the inefficiency of false equality. For too long, we have allowed ourselves to be dragged down by those who contribute nothing. The world has turned its back on us. But we—we will be stronger for it. We will be better. And we will take our rightful place in history."

And the crowds cheered. They wanted to believe him. They wanted to believe in a world where effort meant success. Where work was rewarded, weakness punished. Where the strong ruled because they deserved to rule. Callus called it a meritocracy. The Algorithm—the heart of it all—keeps it running perfectly. It calculates everything, every action. Your work, your spending, your social engagements, your health, your mood, your behavior. And the sum of those factors is your "Socio-Economic Standing". A high score ranks you as a better asset. Lower scores mark you as a lesser asset. And if you are not a score of at least 2.0 you are no longer an asset at all— you become a liability.

I thought about the woman. How she'd wait at that vendor for an hour. She'd watch the crowd, scanning faces, searching for my arrival with the slightest glimmer of hope that maybe, just maybe, I'd keep my word. But eventually, she'd move on, already to aware that I had lied. It's just how things work here. The system had rules.

Work hard. Be efficient. Follow the rules. Your SES Score will rise. Or. Break the rules. Become a burden. Your SES will drop.

"New Columbia will be the greatest nation in history," Callus had said. "Not because we force it to be—but because our people will choose to be great."

But what happens if she wasn't allowed to choose greatness? What if it was not the woman who had failed the system? What if, like me, the system had failed her?

New Columbia is an engine. A massive, living machine, fueled by efficiency, productivity, and obedience. Once your SES drops too low, you lose access to better jobs. Then better housing. Then food. Then you're offloaded. Because dead weight only slows the machine. The bottom never rises. It only sinks. And that was the undeniable threat beneath it all.

The people at the top still pretended the contract was in force. They acted like anyone could rise, that merit still mattered, that the Algorithm is neutral. But I knew better. I've seen that those in the upper tier could override SES scores manually. I've seen high-ranking executives flagged by the Algorithm for inefficiency—only to have their numbers quietly "readjusted" the next day. I knew what Callus would never admit: his perfect system was never designed to lift people up. It was designed to keep them useful. They told us that we had, all of us had agreed to the contract. But the reality is that none of us had ever been given an opportunity to not agree.

I glanced down at my wrist. SES: 2.1.

I blinked, and shook my head, pulling myself out of my thoughts. The morning commuters swirled around me, moving with perfect rhythm—efficient, precise, unfeeling. The city is a living organism. The billboards adjust in real time. The security drones drift overhead, scanning, observing.

Gripping my wrist, I picked up my pace. I have a story to pitch. I have time to fix this. And I can't afford to fail.

Suddenly a sharp alarm pulse cuts through the morning chatter. The noise is cold, sterile, absolute. The kind that stops conversations mid-sentence, that makes every person in its radius straighten instinctively, turning to see who the latest fatality will be. I saw him immediately. Seconds before the drones arrive. A man—mid-forties, shoulders hunched in defeat—stood frozen in place, wristband blinking red. He simply stared at it, as if he could will the number to change. He cannot.

SES: 1.9.

The threshold has been crossed. The Algorithm had decided: he is no longer fit to remain in society. As the drones descended — smoothly, methodically, there was no panic. No confusion. The process played out with the same orderly precision of the rest of the New Columbia. The first drone clamped a restraint around his wrist. The second scanned his ID, confirming what everyone already knew: His value was gone. He doesn't fight. Most of them don't. They know there's no point.

By now, a crowd had gathered, as they always do.

Some watch in silence. Others whisper to each other. A few take out their devices, recording to post on their newsfeed. And then there are the ones who cheer.

"Dead weight!" someone shouts.

A man in a pristine corporate coat, his SES glowing well above 5.0.

"Should've worked harder!"

There are scattered nods from others in the crowd—the ones who've never felt the fear of slipping, the ones who believe in the Contract. I watched the transport drone rise into the sky, carrying away another erased citizen. Most of the people watching simply turned and walked off.

"Show is over and it's time to keep your own score from sinking."

Most never even wonder where the drone has taken this individual. They don't want to know, It's easier to think the system would fix them, somehow. But few people spoke about it.

I have done some research. I spent months pulling records, scraping data, tracking stories that never saw the light of day. Searching for details on the ones who were offloaded. And the deeper I dug, the clearer it became. The Undercity wasn't just a poor-folks home. It wasn't just some nebulous slum where the offloaded lived out the rest of their days in quiet shame. It was a prison. A dumping ground. A feeding pit. A place where life had no value. And death was the only way out.

Worst of all, the Undercity wasn't an accident. It was designed. Planned, constructed, and filled on purpose. Callus' team of architects and corporate strategists—his monsters—had set it aside as a containment sector. A neat little phrase, wrapped in government documentation, hiding a nightmare. The official story? It was a "Productivity Reallocation Zone." A place where the inefficient could find roles more suited to their abilities. The reality? A slave camp where corporations outsourced labor for pennies on the credit.

That was the real joke of it all. Even after being cast out of society, if you were willing to break your back in the factories—if you signed away your body for medical testing—if you gave yourself over to a sex trade that never ran out of buyers—there were still soul-sucking jobs in the Undercity. Everything the "socially fit" pretended didn't exist. And everything they were happy to secretly pay for.

It wasn't money that ruled the Undercity. It was favors. Flesh. Control. It was who you belonged to. If you weren't strong enough to fight, you worked. If you couldn't work, you were sold.

I also discovered that not everyone who was offloaded ended up in the Undercity. Some just simply disappeared. No records. No relocation. No trace. Just gone. And there were rumors. Too many rumors. Usually, it was people who upset the system. Rocked the boat. People like me who went looking for things they shouldn't, asking questions they shouldn't— hackers, ex-officials, rogue enforcers—simply never came back. The joke, the one told in the lower sectors, was that the missing became the "bedrock" of New Columbia.

"Check the footings of the newest luxury towers," someone had once told me over drinks. "The ones they build for the 5.5s and up. You might find your answers there."

I laughed at the time. But now, watching that drone fade into the skyline, I'm not laughing anymore.

The worst part? Everyone seems to know. People just don't talk about it. They don't ask questions. But they know. Every person who clutches their wristband, watching their SES flicker closer to the edge, knows exactly what happens when you fall too far. They just hope it never happens to them. Because if it did? The only way out was down.

The people who cheered and then turned away this morning probably never had to wonder if their number might drop tomorrow. I stare at them, at the casual cruelty of their faces, and wonder if they have ever once felt afraid. As if reading my mind, a man beside me said, "The ones who cheer are the ones who need to be offloaded."

I glanced at him. He's older, late fifties maybe, hair graying at the edges, SES barely above 3.0. He doesn't look at me.

I hesitated, then asked, "so, what do you think happens to them?"

I expected the standard answer—the one we all say when we want to keep our scores stable—is They are given new opportunities suited to their abilities. It's a lie, of course. No one comes back from offload Status. But I ask anyway. Because something about him makes me think he'll give me a different answer. He smiles, but it's the kind that doesn't reach his eyes.

"I think the Undercity is whatever you want it to be."

I blinked, trying to guess what his meaning. "What?"

He gestures toward the empty space where

the transport pod had been, now nothing but an afterthought in the morning routine.

"Some people tell themselves it's a second chance. That the Board reassigns them, gives them new roles out of public view. Others think it's a prison. A labor camp where the inefficient pay off their debts. And some think it's just a hole in the ground, where they dump bodies and rewrite the records."

I swallow. "So which one is it?"

He finally looks at me. His eyes are sharp. "Whichever one lets you sleep at night."

Chapter 3

WILLIAM HOLLIS- EDITOR IN CHIEF

The headquarters of The Truth stands like a monolith of authority—sleek, towering, and immaculate beneath the morning haze. It is the sole voice of information in New Columbia, the only source deemed pure and unquestionable, its reports validated by the Algorithm itself. Anything outside its broadcasts is disregarded, discredited, or erased. Its glass-and-steel exterior is a masterpiece of design—sharp angles and flawless transparency, an illusion of openness masking the absolute control within. The mirrored facade reflects the city back at its people, reinforcing the order, the structure, the world as they are told it exists. Those who pass by see themselves as the Algorithm sees them—polished, compliant, exactly as they should be. But inside, there is no reflection of the citizens. Only the narrative the system wants them to hear.

I stepped through the main plaza outside the building, forcing myself to match the rhythm of the morning crowd. Smile, stand tall, look purposeful. People who look tired, anxious, withdrawn attract attention. And attention is dangerous. Even here, among the city's educated professionals, no one takes chances. The men and women around me greet each other with bright, curated enthusiasm—their expressions a careful balance of corporate ambition and effortless contentment. It's an act. I know it. They know it. But that's the point, isn't it?

Efficiency is happiness.

The Leader himself said so. Everyone plays along. Everyone smiles, laughs, talks about their productivity scores as if they mean something, as if they are anything but a measure of how long they'll be allowed to exist. I did the same, nodding politely as I passed familiar faces. Inside, my disgust curdled.

The lobby of The Truth is a masterpiece of engineered sterility.

Polished black marble, floor-to-ceiling glass panels, a sweeping LED screen that dominates the far wall, cycling through the morning headlines.

CALLUS ANNOUNCES NEW INITIATIVE
TO PROMOTE SOCIAL UNITY
OFFLOADING RATES DROP TO HISTORIC LOWS
PROOF OF SYSTEM SUCCESS
THE FUTURE IS NOW: A.I. PIONEERS NEW ERA
OF TRUSTED INFORMATION

The artificial cheerfulness of the headlines clashes violently with the reality of the building itself. There is no warmth here. No chatter, no spontaneous laughter, none of the forced social pleasantries from outside. Only quiet efficiency. It's as if the moment they step through the doors, the people here are drained of color. Even the receptionists, the few human workers who haven't been replaced, speak in even, mechanical tones. Their smiles—when they do appear—are thin and rehearsed. I recognized the one sitting at the main desk today. She glanced up as I entered, her expression blank but assessing. Her gaze lingered.

I knew why. Her screen recognized me, and she saw my score.

I didn't acknowledge it. Instead, I gave her the same practiced smile as everyone else. She didn't return it. Not really. Just a flicker of acknowledgment before she turned back to her console. I moved toward the elevators, forcing myself to walk with purpose, confidence, and normalcy. Because that's the game. And if you don't play it, you don't last.

There was a time when this place had a pulse. When the newsroom buzzed with human voices, arguments over headlines, the hurried clatter of keys as breaking stories unfolded. Now? Now it is silent. A.I. does everything—the drafting, the editing, the placement of stories, the predictive sentiment analysis that determines which version of the truth the people will accept most easily. There are still a handful of us left. Not because we're needed. But because The Leader understands perception. People want to believe there are humans behind the words they consume. That there is a mind, a soul, a conscience shaping the news they read. So we are allowed to exist.

A handful of writers, sitting at desks that used to be filled with hundreds. We work alongside the AI, reviewing the pre-generated articles, pretending we have any influence over what will be published. The Algorithm now watches every keystroke. Everything we write is processed, analyzed — corrected where necessary. Even the way we phrase our internal notes on a draft is subject to scrutiny. Too many flagged "editorial suggestions" can lead to undesirable consequences. I learned that lesson early. I play along.

I took a deep breath, steadying myself before I stepped into the elevator. I had a meeting to attend. And I must convince my editor that my story—the one that could unravel everything—is just another tribute to the Leader's brilliance.

If I don't pull it off? My SES will drop, and I can't afford another drop.

The conference room is too large for two people. It's designed for twelve—a sleek, glass table stretching across the room, projection screens running the latest headlines, a holo-display embedded in the center for AI-led briefings. But today, it's just Hollis and me. The moment I stepped inside, a sharp wave of unease pulsed through my body, electric and raw. Monday meetings are never enjoyable, but at least they're predictable—the entire team reviewing assignments, debating phrasing, ensuring that every article aligns with the "official narrative."

But today, there is no team. Just William Hollis, Editor-in-Chief of The Truth, sitting alone at the head of the table. The moment he saw me, he smiled— practiced, polished, and utterly hollow. The kind of smile that fits the mouth but just a shade off.

"Iris, come in, have a seat."

Hollis has been in this business for a long time. He built his career before The Algorithm dictated which words were acceptable and which ones were destabilizing. He knows how to project confidence and authority. But right now? He looks tired. Not just end-of-the-day tiredness. More like someone who has seen the edge of something terrible and knows he can't step back. I lowered myself into the chair across from him, forcing my posture to remain neutral. The silence stretches.

Hollis shuffled a pile of papers in front of him, flipping pages like he was looking for something. But he's not reading. It's an old trick. A way to avoid eye contact while he pulls together whatever speech he's rehearsed. I wait. Finally, he sighed pulling a hand slowly over his face.

"So," he said, clearing his throat. "How's the morning treating you?"

I took a moment to wonder why his demeanor was so off. Hollis is not one for small talk, so I don't answer right away. I've been through enough of these conversations to know when someone is stalling.

"Fine," I said carefully.

"Good, good." He nodded, too quickly, obviously not paying attention. I could have told him that I was on fire and gotten the same reply.

"You know, I was just thinking about the first piece you wrote for The Truth—what was it? Five, six years ago?"

"Seven."

"Seven. Damn. Time flies, huh?"

I didn't respond.

Because he isn't reminiscing. He's delaying. He was absent-mindedly bouncing his pencil on the table, contemplating what he was going to say next. His eyes dart toward mine, then away. The air shifts. The illusion breaks. It was clear what was going on. I felt it in my gut before he even spoke the words. But his words don't come easy.

Puffing his cheeks, he let out a slow breath, obviously struggling with his words.

"Listen, Iris… this really kills me, but…"

A pause. Then, with quiet finality:

"Your position is being terminated. Effective immediately."

The words land like a weight I was already braced for—but that didn't make them any lighter. Not "reassigned." Not "contract adjustment." They weren't moving me to another department. They weren't giving me a chance to stabilize my SES. They were cutting me loose.

Terminated.

I let the silence stretch. Waiting. Hollis shifted uncomfortably in his chair.

"You know how this works," his voice still quiet. "The Algorithm flagged you. It's nothing personal."

"It's never personal," I said flatly.

A weak smile. "Right."

I watched him carefully. The way his hands wouldn't stay still. The tension in his shoulders. The fact that he couldn't look at me for more than a few seconds.

"Did you at least go to bat for me?"

Hollis lets out a short, humorless laugh.

"I tried," he lied "I really did. But The Algorithm classified you. The Board described you as a liability, there's nothing I can do."

Liability. A sanitized word for disposable. Hollis hesitated, fingers drumming against the tabletop. Then, for the first time in the conversation, he leaned forward, lowering his voice. He knew full well this entire conversation was being monitored. Hell, the entire building was bugged. He pulled a small device from his shirt pocket and switched it on. I'd seen it before. A jamming device. Not enough to stop the recording of our conversation, but enough to make the words garbled and unintelligible.

"Look… off the record?" His gaze flickered to the tinted windows. "You need to disappear, Iris. Make yourself invisible, before it's too late."

I frowned. "Invisible? What are you talking about?"

"You think this is just about your job?" He shakes his head. "It's not. They don't just erase positions anymore. They erase people. Look at your score Iris."

Something cold curled at the base of my spine.

"They" meant the Board. The Corporate Enforcers. The ones who take the offloaded and make sure they're never heard from again. Hollis reached into the pile of papers in front of him, pulled out a thin folder, and slid it toward me. I hesitated, then flipped it open. My pulse stopped cold. Activity logs. Surveillance notes. Anomalies flagged in my data trail. But what made my stomach knot was the last entry:

Subject exhibits patterns of investigative deviation.
Review of classified data linked to security breach.
Recommended action: Offload Review

I raised my hand to my face, fingers pressing into my forehead, turning the page. Surveillance photos. Of me. Stepping into my apartment. Sitting at a café. Talking to a source from my last report. Then the last page—a list of names. Journalists. Activists. Former colleagues. Some of them I know. Some have already disappeared.

I looked at Hollis. "How long have you had this?"

He didn't answer. My fingers tighten around the edges. Possession of classified data linked to security breach. Proof that my score didn't drop due to some missed payment or forgotten social protocol. I flip through the pages again, slower this time.

One image catches my eye. A grainy, black-and-white shot of me sitting at an outdoor café. Taken from a distance and enlarged too many times. It takes me a moment to place it—taken just days ago. The day I had gained access to the Algorithm's data, looking for any unreported data files. Suddenly I recognize someone else in the photo. Sitting at a table just a few meters behind me. The same man from this morning. The one who stood beside me as we watched some poor bastard get offloaded.

"The ones who cheer are the ones who need to be offloaded."

He had looked so ordinary. Just another tired worker, blending into the crowd. But now, — frozen in the photograph, weeks before I even knew his face — he'd been watching me. I flipped through the other surveillance photos, my breath tightening. He appeared again. Never obvious—sometimes in the background, sometimes in passing. But always nearby.

I inhaled slowly, forcing myself to stay calm. Maybe he had just happened to live nearby, near enough to show up in the same places by chance. But that was the problem, wasn't it? In New Columbia, there is no chance. Everything—every route, every schedule, every interaction—is tracked, analyzed, predicted. The Algorithm knows where you are going before you do. And now, someone else does too.

I closed the folder. Pushed it back across the desk.

Hollis frowns. "Iris—"

"I knew I was treading on thin ice," I said. "Now I know how much..."

A flicker of frustration crosses his face.

"You don't get it," he interrupted, leaning in. "They won't stop until they've made you disappear."

I studied him. The old Bill Hollis - the editor who once believed in chasing the truth no matter the cost— was gone. In his place was a man who had learned to survive. For a moment I considered listening to him. I could run. Disappear into the system, like the others.

But then he said something that set off alarms in my head.

"They'll find the files eventually Iris, you know that, right?"

My files. How the hell did he know about the files? Is he the leak? Has Hollis set me up? My mind swirls. If he has, will he let me walk out?

"Tell you what, Bill," I said, pushing the folder into my purse, "let me wrap my head around this. I'll get back to you in bit."

And I walked out the door.

I stepped out of The Truth's headquarters, the glass doors sliding shut behind me with a quiet hiss. The morning rush still pulses through the city. The rhythm of work schedules, transit routes, programmed efficiency. I walk, keeping my pace steady, controlled. But inside, my thoughts are spinning out of control.

"You need to disappear, Iris. Make yourself invisible."

That's what Hollis had said. Disappear. But to where? There is nowhere to go outside the confines of this damned place. New Columbia is the last functioning city-state—the only place left after the global collapse. The old governments crumbled under hyperinflation, resource wars, uncontrolled automation. The world's economy fractured beyond repair. One by one, cities fell into chaos. Until only New Columbia stood. It alone had managed to survive because we alone had embraced order, structure, and The Algorithm. And there was no escaping from it.

"They'll find the files eventually Iris, you know that, right?"

Hollis knew I was holding classified files, but it didn't add up. The folder mentioned the security breach but made no mention of the files. But Hollis had mentioned them specifically. How could he know? Was he guessing, or was he privy to info even the Algorithm hadn't picked up on yet?

The long walk back to my apartment felt different now. Not because the streets had changed—they hadn't. The same holo-ads adjusted in real-time, flashing promotions designed to appeal to me specifically. The same security drones drifted overhead, scanning the crowd for signs of non-compliance. They'd always been a part of my life, nothing to be feared if you had nothing to hide. But now, I felt it. The quiet watching. The knowledge that every step, every turn, every breath is calculated by a system that has already decided I am obsolete.

So why hadn't they offloaded me immediately?

And then—the answer hits me. They need the files. I had proof, months of investigations into SES manipulations, forced offload patterns, and how the Algorithm is being manipulated by the Oligarchs. By now they had erased the original data, covering their tracks. Except—

I still had a copy.

I had been careful. Methodical. Hidden my work behind encrypted firewalls. Took advantage of air-gapped data silos. And now they needed access to what I have. They can't cover their tracks as long as I have the data. A chill ran down my spine. They fired me today. Which means they know it's not on files at the Truth. And that means—I pick up my pace—they'll be looking for them in my apartment.

By the time I reach home, my heartbeat is a

dull hammer behind my ribs. The door scans my ID without hesitation—no security locks, no failed clearance. That means they haven't been here yet. I step inside. Stop. My heart skips a beat.

Someone's been here and they were thorough. Drawers pulled open. Hard drives gone. Data slates missing. My workstation—a customized, air-gapped rig—sits powered down, the casing cracked open. Whoever had been here, they weren't subtle. They wanted me to see this. Wanted me to know they had taken everything. My files. My backups. Every record I had ever collected. All of it—wiped clean.

They took everything. Everything—except the drive in my pocket. My fingers tightened around it. A small, encrypted thumb drive no bigger than my thumbnail. The one I had carried with me today, out of habit. The one that held the raw data I hadn't even had time to parse yet. The one they had been looking for. And they hadn't found it. Not yet.

I almost laughed. Then I felt a buzz on my wrist. A notification from the system. A single message, displaying my SAS score:

SES: 2.0

My score had just dropped again. One step away from being offloaded.

Chapter 4

STEP INTO CONFUSION

I kept thinking about the guy in the photo. Was he an agent with the System? Surely, they would have sent an enforcer, not an undercover agent. But then again, he hadn't looked like someone who would be standing in the crowd watching a poor soul be offloaded. His coat was old, but not ragged. His shoes are worn but not ruined. His SES wasn't high—just above 3.0, enough to survive but never thrive. Most people at his level keep their heads down. They don't watch. And they certainly don't make comments to strangers. But he had.

"The ones who cheer are the ones who need to be offloaded."

It sounded conspiratorial. Not exactly the kind of remark to make to a stranger in the streets of New Columbia, where SES scores can go up for reporting anti-social actors. But he wasn't exactly a stranger either, was he? He was in the photos. He'd been following me. Was this an attempt to contact me as a conspirator? Or was this his way of baiting me to admit something?

I had no idea who he was. But I did not trust him. That thought got me thinking about someone else I didn't know anything about--the man whose identity I had used to gain access into the system. I'd done my homework on him. Adam Solace. He used to be someone well connected. A developer, a systems engineer, a man who had written the security protocols for the Algorithm. SES: 6.1. He had a penthouse in the Inner District. He had a view of the skyline. He had a wife who adored him and a daughter who was going to get her first SES evaluation in six months. And then— he had disappeared.

I traced his log entries back and found his last entry was a routine database audit. Probably clearing redundancies, eliminating old profiles, tidying the system. That's when he must have seen it. He wasn't supposed to have access to offload records, but somehow, he had slipped past a firewall. Records of missing people. offloaded citizens with log entries ending with: "Asset Terminated." No record of delivery into the Undercity. Outside the System, one might say murdered. But in a government setting, assassination comes to mind. Either way, this Adam Solace had left me a clue.

I had followed his trail the same way I followed any story lead—through patterns, inconsistencies, the cracks where truth slips through. And now I realized that he and I were suddenly on the same path. These records refelcted a dark secret. Evidence that our 'perfect' Algorithm was practing social-cleansing by systematically deleting it's undesirable population.

His SES score had been even better than my own— a solid 6.1, a man with security, privilege, a future.

His records painted a perfect citizen. And then, like mine, his SES took a sudden dive. Not the kind that comes from poor performance, bad spending habits, or a string of unfortunate social connections. This was a deliberate removal. Although there were no strikes against him, his records indicated he was flagged for 'Recalibration'.

That word sent a chill through me. It wasn't a demotion. It wasn't a reassessment. Recalibration meant something much worse. Recalibration meant overwriting neural pathways. It meant stripping a person's brain of identity. Recalibration wasn't a correction; it was a the quiet destruction of a mind. And when it was finished, when there was nothing left of the person they used to be, the system marked them with those final, chilling words:

FINAL ASSET PROCESS COMPLETE.

A bureaucratic epitaph. The last record of someone who no longer existed. But in his case, like the others he had been looking for, there was no corresponding record of him having been sent to the Undercity. Just the entry "Final Asset Process Complete." He'd been poking around these files and now suddenly he was gone.Everything about Adam Solace stopped—cold. No termination notice. No final logins. No flagged bank transactions or pension reallocation. Just… absence. Whoever Adam Solace was before, he wasn't that person anymore.

I kept digging. What I found was a ghost. The system had failed to remove him entirely. Fragments of a profile left untouched; credentials still active—

an identity wiped from the system's consciousness but never properly deleted. I suddenly realized I had stumbled into a perfect blind spot. An opportunity too good to ignore. I realized that if the Algorithm didn't register his demise nor his existence, then neither would anyone else. His access codes were still valid, his clearance level still intact—a door left unlocked. I decided I would step through it.

I still had my credentials—my identity as Iris Delacroix, Senior Investigative Journalist, was intact. The Algorithm trusted me, at least then. That was the advantage of working for The Truth—press clearance came with access, and access was everything. But my clearance only went so deep. Officially, my level was capped at 4.3. Just enough to review public records, cross-reference historical archives, and pull reports from the city's SES databases. It let me query the system, but it didn't let me see it. Not really. Not like I needed to.

I had to go deeper.

Breaking into a system governed by a post-singularity intelligence was no cake-walk—there were no brute-force exploits, no human-made backdoors, no predictable flaws in the code. The Algorithm was always learning. It adapted. It identified and patched vulnerabilities long before human minds even knew they existed. But there was one thing it still didn't fully understand. Betrayal of trust.

The Algorithm operated on absolute logic, 'yes or no', built on layers of permissions and access trees, each step requiring verification from a higher, trusted source. Who you are determines what you can see. It doesn't question motive. I exploited that. I could give it a reason for my being there. A reason to be looking. I was aware that accessing a restricted file outright would trigger security flags. Every action needed authorization, and authorization required a Security Principal. A human fail-safe in a system built to be perfect. I let the system do what it was designed to do.

I searched for a file just outside my clearance level. Just high enough that requesting access would look routine—something an investigative journalist might need for an approved report. A necessary overstep.

ACCESS DENIED

I expected that. But the system had a fail-safe for people like me—employees who worked under direct supervision. A function built for junior analysts, assistants, and interns. I typed in the command

→ *req.temp.acc\security.principal*

I hesitated. Then hit enter.

The system did what it was designed to do—it pinged the assigned authority for this level of access. One Adam Solace.

His credentials were still in the system, still marked as active, still tied to a person the Algorithm believed existed. The system sent the request, and Adam Solace—who wasn't there to deny it—approved my access. Because I had just become him.

Not through a brute-force hack. Not through password cracking or bypassing bio-metric scans. I had done it the way the system allowed—by following protocol. By being patient. By letting the Algorithm trust me. I allowed the Algorithm to believe the process had been verified. That all players could be trusted to be who they presented themselves as. It assigned a temporary clearance override, just enough to let the request go through. I had exactly eleven and half minutes before the temporary access window would close and that override would be purged from the logs—an automatic correction, a self-healing process. No human eyes would ever see it.

Once inside, I chained requests, each one piggybacking off the last, tricking the system into assuming I was exactly where I was supposed to be. Security isn't just about access. It's about expectation. The Algorithm saw the user following a pre-approved workflow. I never forced my way in. I never broke protocol. I just let the Algorithm believe I belonged there.

Which is how I found the tampered records. The files showing human interference in a perfect algorithm. And these were the very files they wanted returned.

But who was Adam Solace and where was he now. That was the real anomaly.

Chapter 5

CAPT. EVELYN RAYNE - ISB ENFORCER

Iris Delecroix's apartment was taped off when I arrived at the building. Several officers are milling about. A sergeant recognizes me and holds up a hand indicating he is the incident command leader. I approached him.

"Officer Rayne?" he asked.

"Yes, sergeant" I replied. "I take it the place is vacant."

"Correct, looks like someone beat us to the punch."

"Damn. Mind if I have a look?"

The sergeant motioned me towards the doorway. "We've been expecting you. You now have incident command" He stepped back from the doorway allowing me to pass through.

The apartment is small. Smaller than I expected. I stepped inside, the echo of my boots swallowing the silence. The air carried the faint scent of coffee, of paper, of someone who lived in a world of words instead of actions. I scanned the room—bed unmade, desk cluttered with notes, walls bare except for a single, framed photo on the shelf. No excess. No waste. But no discipline, either. She lived like a woman who never expected to be caught.

The enforcers moved behind me, methodical,

precise. Drawers yanked open, cabinets overturned, a tablet smashed to pieces on the floor. But it wasn't them. The damage was old—minutes, maybe hours. Someone had already been here.

I crouched, running my fingers over the jagged shards of the broken tablet. Already wiped. Already worthless. But the destruction was messy, desperate. Someone had been looking for something. Something they hadn't found.

A lifetime of searching had taught me one thing: people like Iris Delacroix never leave the truth where you expect to find it. She wasn't stupid. But she was arrogant. And arrogance left footprints. Behind me, one of the sergeants scoffed.

"Looks like she trashed the place herself. Covered her tracks before we got here."

I exhaled sharply, rising to my feet.

"No," I said, scanning the wreckage again. "This wasn't her." I scanned the room. "Someone else is looking for the same thing we are."

I thought for a moment, briefly considering who it might be that wanted the info we were after. Who else had interest and knowledge of the files? By the looks of it, they were not allies. Iris had fled in a hurry. And that meant the files still existed somewhere. If—no — when—I find Iris I will figure out who is involved and will put an end to this nonsense.

Iris Delacroix thinks she is above the system. I have read her work. The lies she has already smuggled through the cracks in the system, the half-truths she weaves into the minds of weaker people who trust the

Truth. I have seen the way she poisons them—how she makes them believe they are victims—not liabilities.

Headline: Improvements to Algorithm eliminate error: suggesting "The Algorithm is not infallible."
Headline: Adjusted program identifies new security threats: implying "New Columbia citizens are not safe."
Nonsense. All of it.

She is not trying to help us. She is trying to cast doubts to weaken our resolve. I closed my eyes for a brief moment, steadying my thoughts. The past is a locked door, but sometimes it creaks open when I am not careful. I remember my father's face—the way he looked when they took him.

"The system isn't fair," he had said, voice quiet, shaking. "It's broken, Evelyn. Don't let them make you think it's your fault."

I was twelve. I remember watching him being offloaded. I remember my mother holding my shoulders, gripping them too tightly, forcing me to stand still and watch.

"This is what happens to people who don't try hard enough."

He had tried. He just hadn't been good enough. And I would never be him. I open my eyes. The apartment around me is just another symptom of the disease. Callus was right. Weakness is not just failure. It is contagion. And people like Iris Delacroix? They are carriers.

The leader's words still ring in my mind, steady

and unshakable.

"The Algorithm is the mind. But we, the loyal, are the hand."

We are not just enforcers. We are the blade that cuts away the rot. I remember the first time I saw him in person. His voice filled the chamber, controlled, measured, absolute. He did not shout, did not need to. He spoke, and the weak listened. The strong understood.

"Perfection is not given. It is earned. And those who resist perfection are enemies of the future."

Some called him ruthless. Some called him a tyrant. I called him necessary. New Columbia is not broken. It is not some decaying ruin, the way Iris and her kind want people to believe. But it is unfinished. And I will do whatever it takes to see his vision realized. Even if it means burning the past to the ground.

The enforcers finished sweeping through the apartment. Nothing useful. But it doesn't matter. The hunt has already begun. I press my thumb against my comm-link.

"Activate citywide tracking. She's running. I want every drone scanning the Undercity exits."

A pause. Then: "Captain, her SES has been flagged. If she tries to go through a secure exit, we'll be notified."

I allowed myself a smile—small and sharp. "She won't be using secure exits" I mumble to myself.

She is smart. But she is a woman who spent too long in the light, thinking the dark could never touch her. Now, I am the dark. And I am coming for her. But the reality is not lost on me. She is on the run, and we have not found her here. Until one of the security drones picks up her signal, there is nothing I can do.

It's been a long day. My cat is probably wondering where I am. I thought to myself.

I made my way through the streets of New Columbia on my way home. I love how people step aside, almost bowing at my presence. My helmet and face shield keep them from seeing the smile on my face as they push up against walls so as not to stand in my way. I am the body of fear. I am why they obey. They do not want to see me in their daily activities. If you see me involved in your day, you are probably having a bad day.

Reaching my building, I pushed through the outer doors. The door slid shut behind me, sealing out the noise of the city. I pressed my palm to the entry scanner. The apartment came to life—lights flickered on, temperature adjusting, the soft mechanical clicks of locks re-engaging. Order. Structure. Control. I inhaled deeply, savoring the silence. No wasted space. No unnecessary distractions. Just clean lines, neutral tones, everything exactly where it should be. The bed, made with military precision. The kitchen, minimalist and spotless. My terminal aligned perfectly at the center of my desk. A place where nothing is out of place.

A soft chirp breaks the silence. Then a weight curled around my leg. I glanced down. Milo, my sleek, gray cat winds between my boots, tail flicking in irritation, golden eyes narrowing as if judging me for being late.

"Stop that," I muttered, stepping over him as I moved toward the kitchen. He follows, making a low, impatient sound.

I sighed. "Fine. You first."

I pulled a small dish from the cabinet, measured out his portion of nutrient-enriched kibble, and set it down. He sniffed it once before settling into his meal, tail curled neatly around his paws. Only then did I allow myself to relax a bit, tension leaking from my shoulders. I reached for a meal packet from the cooling unit, scanning the label out of habit—balanced macros, optimized for performance, no excess carbohydrates—before placing it in the heating unit. Eighteen seconds to perfection.

The cat, now satisfied, jumped onto the countertop.

"You have no discipline."

He flicked an ear. Ignoring me. Of course he did. His name was Milo—a name I did not chose. He had belonged to someone before me. A woman I barely remember, one of the Academy instructors, a rare one who had spoken softly. She had died when I was seventeen. I don't know how, and I never asked. But when they cleared out her quarters, no one took the cat. I had. And to this day I don't know why. I don't like pets, normally.

But Milo is OK.

I leaned against the counter as my meal finished heating, eyes drifting to the single window in my apartment. The city stretched beyond endlessly—

orderly, brilliant, and cold. Glass towers and glowing walkways, the soft blue pulse of data streams in the sky. From here, it looked perfect. Because it is meant to.

Iris Delacroix would never understand that. She and the others - the failures, the weak, the selfish - they saw the walls of New Columbia and called it a prison. I saw the walls and thought of them as protection. People like Iris had not grown up the way I had. They did not know what it meant to hunger for something better.

I remembered the way my mother had rationed food, measuring out calories like they were currency. I can remember watching her sell the last of my father's possessions, just to keep our SES score from dipping lower. I remember the shame.

The Academy had taken me in when I was thirteen. They had given me a uniform, a schedule, a purpose. I learned discipline, strength, and structure. And the hunger? It had vanished. The weak called it brutal. I called it correction. We rose before dawn, synchronized in movement, our schedules optimized to the second. Our failures were punished immediately, without hesitation, because hesitation was a weakness.

They had stripped away my name—at first. Not as punishment, but as a test.

"A name is nothing without value," the instructors had told us. "Earn your place. Earn your identity."

They had rebuilt me. And I am better for it.

The heating unit beeped, pulling me from my thoughts. I retrieved the meal, sat at my small, bare table, and begin eating. Each bite calculated, each movement practiced, the same way I had done since the Academy.

Milo jumped onto the table, watching me. I ignored him.

Instead, my thoughts returned to Iris. She would never see the world the way I did. To her, rules were shackles, not structure. Order was something to defy, not embrace. She called the system oppression, when it had given her everything. And now, she was running from it.

A slow burn of frustration coiled in my chest. Not at myself. Not at the failure to find her files. But at her. At all of them. They were too soft to survive on their own, too fragile to endure the reality of an optimized world—so instead, they call it evil. They live in the dark, spreading their decay to others, making them believe the system itself is cruel. But which is more cruel? Watching people fail on their own? Or guiding them—forcing them—to be better?

Callus understood this. He saw what needed to be done.

Perfection is not given. It is earned.

The city's systems were already working. Tracking her. Filtering possibilities. She might try to disappear, but the Algorithm sees deeper. Her habits. Her movements. Her inefficiencies. She would make a mistake. These types always did. And when she did? I would be there.

Milo stretched out on the table, curling into himself, eyes half-lidded. At ease. Unburdened. I studied him for a long moment.

"You're lucky you don't have to think about these things," I murmured.

His tail flicked. He gave a slow blink. Dismissive. I allowed myself the smallest smile. Then, as quickly as it came, I let it fade. Tomorrow, the hunt would continue.

The next morning, I walked to my favorite coffee shop. It is a short five-minute walk down the clean and well-manicured streets. The café is pristine. Of course it is. Smooth glass, polished steel, rows of neatly spaced tables, all identical in size. The scent of freshly brewed coffee fills the air—real coffee, not the synthetic blends reserved for lower-tier districts. Every worker moves with silent precision, their uniforms crisp, their movements optimized. No wasted time. No wasted space. Perfect efficiency. This is how the world was meant to be.

I settled into my seat across from Lieutenant Marion Voss, one of the few enforcers I trust. She was already sipping her coffee, eyes scanning the latest updates on her tablet. Her expression was pleasant, her movements relaxed—the look of a woman who knew the system was working. I held my own cup, letting the warmth seep into my fingers. A rare moment of calm. A reward earned.

"You saw the broadcast?" Marion asked without looking up.

I nodded, taking a slow sip. Dark roast. No sugar, no excess. "Of course."

Marion smiled. "Brilliant, wasn't it?"

It had been. Chancellor Callus had spoken just before sunrise, his voice steady, controlled—the voice of reason in an imperfect world. He had announced the latest milestone in The Great Optimization.

"We have nearly eradicated the last remnants of disorder. The final restructuring will be complete within the year."

"New Columbia is no longer infected by the old world's corruption."

"We have ensured safety. We have ensured purity."

I stood at attention as I listened, absorbing every word. The rest of the city had as well. Because when Callus spoke, the weak listened. The strong understood. Marion's voice dropped slightly, just enough to keep the conversation private.

"Have you seen the revised stability reports? Incidents of ideological deviation have dropped another 14% this quarter."

I studied her face, the way the low light caught in the fine angles of her cheekbones, the curve of her lips resting between thoughts. There was always something unreadable in her expression, a quiet intensity that made me ache to know her completely. She had loosened her collar slightly, the fabric of her coat still damp from the rain, and I could see the faintest crease where her brow had furrowed earlier, a trace of the weight she carried in her position as enforcer.

"The system is working."

She nodded. "We're close now. Another few cycles and we'll have full compliance."

Full compliance. The thought sent a slow, quiet satisfaction through my chest. Another famous Callus quote ran through my mind.

"Perfection is not given. It is earned."

And we are earning it.

Outside the café, a small crowd was gathering. Silent. Watching. I turn slightly, watching through the clean glass. A pair of enforcers stood at the curb, restraining a man in plain clothes. He wasn't resisting—he didn't dare. Within minutes, he would be gone. Deleted. Corrected.

Marion watched as well, but her expression was unmoved. "Another one."

I nodded. "Another liability to society removed."

She sighed, shaking her head. "A shame. But necessary."

Necessary. That was the word we always used. The word that justified everything. New Columbia had once suffered under a plague of weakness. Crime, disease, social decay—chaos disguised as freedom. For years, criminals and degenerates had poured through the old borders, infesting the city, corrupting its progress. But Callus had changed that. We had changed that.

"You remember the riots?" Marion mused, stirring her coffee. "Before the borders were sealed?"

Who could forget. They had poured in droves, swarming the city like insects. They called themselves refugees, but they had been nothing more than leeches, thieves, parasites—fleeing the collapse of their own failed societies, looking to infect ours with their disease. They had the nerve to demand rights. Demand access. Demand that we let them live among us, polluting our streets with their chaos, their perversions. I remember the reports. Murder. Theft. Rape. And when we finally fought back, when Callus took power and purged them from the city, they cried out. "Oppression. Fascism".

Marion scoffed. "Some people forget what it was like before. How bad things were. How much we suffered."

I nodded. "They don't want to remember. They want to pretend our strength was their problem."

Marion leaned back slightly.

"I have to admit, I had my doubts when Callus first proposed the full restructuring."

I raise an eyebrow. "You?"

She gives a small chuckle. "I know. But you must admit—it wasn't easy, even for us. The correction programs, the restructuring. The last few years have been… necessary, yes, but not painless."

I study her, measuring the weight behind her words. There was no doubt in her voice, but something else lingered there. A memory, perhaps. A hesitation she would never speak aloud. We all had them. I thought of my father, the way his hands had shaken before they took him. I thought of the night we raided the orphanage, clearing out the children who would never meet compliance. I thought of the screams from the detention centers, the way they faded into silence over time. Not painless. But necessary.

"We are stronger for it," I say simply.

Marion agrees. "That we are."

She lifts her coffee cup slightly. A quiet toast. I mirror the motion, the two of us sealing the moment with a shared understanding. We had done what needed to be done. No one else could have. And the city was better for it. She looked at me then, expectant, her fingers brushing absently along the rim of her empty cup. Marion never fidgeted—except with coffee cups, a rare tell in someone so precise. I wanted to reach across the table, still her hands with mine, hold the moment there between us. Instead, I curled my fingers into my sleeve and forced a deep breath.

Marion set down her empty cup. "So. What's your next move on Delacroix?"

My stomach tenses at the name. Iris. She was still out there. Somewhere. The thought unsettled me more than it should have. The longer she remained hidden, the more her lies can be spread. I exhaled slowly, controlling the frustration before it could surface.

"Delacroix," I said, as if the name had completely slipped my mind. "We track her movements. She's still human. She will need food. Shelter. Connection. And that makes her predictable."

Marion looked at me, head slightly tilted. "You're enjoying this, aren't you?"

I felt the warmth of a smile before I let it show, carefully measured, controlled. Anything more would be dangerous. I could never let her see the full truth—the way her voice formed my name, the way I memorized every flicker of expression on her face as if it were the only thing keeping me tethered. I let the smallest of smiles slip through, just enough to keep my feelings for her intact.

"She thinks she's free," I said, leaning forward slightly. "She isn't."

Marion's eyes showed a glint of amusement. "I'll bet a week's rations you find her before the next cycle."

I smiled back. "Make it two."

"Done," she chuckled.

I leaned back in my chair, savoring the quiet moment, the last few sips of bitter coffee. Then I stood to go.

"I have work to do."

Marion set her cup down. "Don't have too much fun without me."

I stepped outside, back into the flawless order of New Columbia. Out here, there was no room for hesitation, no space for anything soft. Love was a liability. And in this city, liabilities got people killed. I walked on, keeping my pace steady, my expression blank, my feelings for Marion a carefully guarded secret.

"Iris Delacroix will make a mistake. And when she does—I'll be there."

Chapter 6

IRIS ON THE RUN

After discovering my apartment had been trashed, I crept down the fire escape into the alley. Sweat began to build on my brow as I started at every noise, every unexpected motion. The enforcers must have been watching my place, why hadn't they grabbed me?

Just then, I saw them streak past, headed to my place. I press my back against the damp brick, forcing myself to breathe slowly, quietly. The rain has started again, a thin drizzle that glistens under the streetlights, turning the pavement slick. Across the street, enforcers move with mechanical precision, their black-clad forms cutting through the neon haze. They're sealing the block.

A barricade unfolds with a hiss, metal barriers locking into place as yellow crime tape unfurls in tight, practiced motions. No hesitation. No questions. Just orders followed. My apartment—what's left of it— is at the center of it all. One of the enforcers gestures to the others, obviously their commanding officer, I could see the set of her shoulders, the careful way she surveys the scene.

My mind swooned again at the sudden realization. Something isn't right. The timing doesn't make sense.

The enforcers are efficient, methodical. They lock a place down before they breach. But my apartment was already torn apart. I saw the shattered monitors, the broken hard drives, the way my door hung slightly off its hinges. And if the enforcers are only just now arriving…that meant...

Someone else had been there first.

A cold, sick feeling curls in my gut. I was so focused on outrunning them that I didn't stop to ask the real question. Who else wanted these files? I replay the scene in my mind—the apartment in ruins, Hollis saying they'd find them, the stranger on the street cryptically speaking to me in riddles.

The rain dripped from my hair, ran down my spine, but the real chill is the one spreading through my chest. If it was just the enforcers, I knew the game. Knew the rules. But this? This was something unexpected. I swallowed against the rising panic, forcing my breathing to calm. I needed to move. I needed to disappear. But the thought gnawed at me, clawing its way through my ribs. Who got there first?

My mind went back to the man in the photos. Was he from the Board? One of the enforcers or an Oligarch henchman? Someone had been in my apartment. And the photos Hollis had given me clearly showed he had been nearby the whole time. Everything in New Columbia was order. Precision. Predictability. Coincidence didn't exist.

And suddenly, as if on cue, there he was.

I spotted him near the transit hub—a gray-haired man, late fifties, hands in pockets, standing too still in the constant movement. He didn't look at me. Not directly. But he was there. Just as he had been there before. At the offloading. In surveillance photos. In my past, without me even knowing. Now, he was in my present. And that was a little too close for comfort.

I veered down a side street, slipping past a row of corporate cafés where professionals laughed at approved jokes and sipped their efficiency-boosting supplements. I didn't turn around. Didn't slow down. Just kept moving with purpose. I fought off the urge to run. Running would set off alarms, but I walked like a person on a mission. A mission to get away from whoever this guy was.

The path opened into a pedestrian plaza, fountains spraying in controlled arcs, the streets impossibly clean, the air thick with the scent of engineered floral arrangements. I risked a glance back. Pausing as if to check out the sale items featured in a storefront. A casual glance down the path I had just come. No sign of him. My muscles eased—maybe I lost him.

Then I turned the corner—

Standing at a tram stop, hands still in his pockets, eyes on nothing in particular. As if he'd been there all along. My skin went cold.

No. That's not possible.

I turned sharply down another street, stepping into a steady stream of pedestrians, letting the crowd swallow me. Through another block. A marketplace this time. Artificial sunlight filtered through the domed ceiling as people browsed vendor kiosks for overpriced luxury items. I wove through them, past the scent of roasted soy proteins and freshly roasted nuts. Another turn.

And there he was again.

Across the street now. Not looking at me. Not moving toward me. Just present. Like a fixed point in the city. Waiting? For me?

My heart hammered.

"Breathe. Think."

This wasn't just tracking. He wasn't chasing me. He was already where I was going. Like I was chasing him. How? Was he reading my movements? Anticipating them? Was The Algorithm telling him where I'd go next? Or worse— Had he already known where I would go? I pushed forward, picking up speed, ducking into a corporate complex with artificial parks, crossing a bridge over a self-cleaning canal. I doubled back, took the mag-line toward a commercial sector, got off early, cut through an open-concept atrium, descended an escalator— And still, every time, he was nearby.

Standing at a storefront. Leaning against a railing. Adjusting his coat in front of a window. Always close. Never following. But never gone. It wasn't normal. It wasn't possible. And yet, it was happening.

I needed to break the pattern. I needed to disappear. I cut left, no thought, no planning—just instinct. A darkened doorway loomed ahead, and I slipped inside.

The air smelled of aged wood and something smoky, like old books and burnt sugar. The heavy door shut behind me with a muted thud, sealing me in.

The space was empty. For a moment I felt dizzy... confused. Luckily no-one was there to see it. I put my hand on a chair to steady myself.

A mechanical clock ticked steadily from somewhere unseen.

I took a slow step forward, scanning the room. The bar stretched the length of the space—solid mahogany, its surface polished to a mirror-like sheen, reflecting the low, amber glow of recessed lighting. Every inch of it spoke of craftsmanship, of a time when things were built to last. Behind it, shelves of expensive-looking liquors stood in perfect order, bottles of deep greens and browns and golds, each label a promise of something illicit and strong. The mirrors lining the back wall reflected nothing but empty chairs and tables, ghostly and still.

Crystal tumblers, cut with intricate facets, were stacked neatly along the lower back-bar, along with an array of bar tools—silver-plated stirrers, old-fashioned muddling mallets, a lined row of knives resting on a wooden cutting board, their edges gleaming in the dim light. It was a place out of time. A relic. And it was completely empty. I exhaled, letting my shoulders ease. I hadn't even realized how tightly I'd been holding myself. No crowd. No movement. No flickering glimpse of him. Maybe I'd finally lost him.

I walked toward the bar, the sound of my own footsteps strangely loud against the wooden floors. I slid onto a stool, facing the rows of bottles instead of the door, willing my mind to stop spinning, to stop analyzing every shadow and every movement outside.

I spread my hands out on the solid wooden bar, feeling the smooth polished wood cool the palms of my had,

I had been there a few minutes before the door at the back of the bar clicked open.

A man stepped out, rolling up the sleeves of his slate-gray button-down. His face was pleasant, calm, like someone used to listening to people. He wasn't surprised to see me. Without a word, he stepped behind the bar, picked up a crystal glass, and began polishing it with a cloth. His movements were slow. Unhurried. He took his time, cleaning the glass in his towel as if it was the most natural thing in the world. The clock continued ticking.

Then, finally he spoke. "Rough day?"

His voice was smooth, calm. I met his gaze, something about his eyes vaguely familiar, but I dismissed it.

I exhaled, forcing my pulse to settle.

"Yeah, you could say that."

He smiled slightly, setting the glass down.

"Whiskey?" he offered.

I nodded. He reached beneath the counter and poured a measure of something amber and expensive looking. Real whiskey, not synthetic. I didn't know they even made it anymore. He didn't ask me to show my wrist or scan my credentials. I didn't offer, knowing it would be denied. I took the glass without a word, my fingers tight around it. Silence stretched between us. I glanced over my shoulder at the door for third time, half expecting the man to be seated next to me by now.

"Waiting for someone?" the bartender asked without looking up from his polishing.

My grip stiffened. I looked up. The bartender raised his eyes to mine, watching me closely.

He pointed towards the door with his chin and added "you keep looking at the door."

"Not waiting," I said carefully. Then thought to myself, "Avoiding."

The bartender huffed a quiet laugh as if he'd heard my thoughts.

"Don't worry. He's not going to follow you in here."

I raised my eyebrows unconsciously. "What does that mean?"

"Means he's not exactly following you. I didn't..." the bartender stopped short and corrected himself ... "he thinks you're just not ready to meet him yet," he said simply.

My blood ran cold. I turned sharply toward the door— Still closed. No sign of him. Slowly, I looked back at the bartender.

He set the glass carefully on a shelf and picked up another from the sink. I watched in silence as he was obviously trying to gather the words together.

"His name is Adam Solace."

The name slams into me like a freight train. I assumed he was dead. Well, apparently not. I tried not to show my reaction.

"Yeah? Well, he's been following me," I said, "for several weeks."

The bartender shook his head. "No. If Adam was

following you, you'd never know it."

I hesitated. My mind was reeling, trying to establish what had happened that I was having this conversation. Something shifted in the air between us. My vision blurred a bit then came back. I was still feeling a little light-headed. And suddenly, it dawned on me that this bartender, whom I had never seen in my life, was chatting with me like we were old friends. As if he knew me. And had just admitted that he knew who was chasing me.

"Ok, and me?" I pressed. "I suppose you already know me too, don't you?"

Another nod. My stomach dropped. I swallowed hard, my throat dry.

"How?" I muttered. "Why." I tried to shake the fuzziness out of my head. This whole thing felt like a dream.

He tilted his head slightly, as if considering his answer. Then, he simply shrugged.

"You know this city; anyone can know anything if they have the right connections. I'm just saying you've got the wrong idea about Adam," he said. "He's not who you think he is."

I stiffened. Confusing thoughts ran through my head. *Anyone can know anything.* I think about what I do know. A disappeared man has been following me, I have been terminated from my ability to raise my SES. My apartment ransacked, obviously Hollis knows about my files. My SES on the brink of getting me offloaded. And now the bartender knows who I am and the name of the man that has been following me.

I glanced around me; was it just happenstance that I came in here? Or had it been planned? What is this place? I don't remember seeing a place that served real alcohol in years. *Alcohol is a weakness* the propaganda posters insisted. I began to look closer at the details of this bar. There are no obvious cameras or surveillance mics. No reminders of the Board or the leader. Nothing that said this place is part of the system.

"It's safe here," the bartender remarked, bringing me back to the present.

"OK, so I have the wrong idea. What's the right idea?"

The bartender gave me a measured look but said nothing.

"Is he government?" I pressed. "Corporate? A freelancer?"

Nothing.

"Well? What's next?"

At that, the bartender grinned. "You'll have to ask him yourself."

I sat looking at him for a long moment. Several questions churned in my mouth, but I didn't release them. I still struggled to grasp what I was hearing. Suddenly I panicked. I stood from the bar stool too quickly, my head still spinning from the conversation. None of this made sense. The bartender knew Adam. He knew me. This place, this bar - a bar that shouldn't exist - wasn't just a coincidence. None of this was coincidence.

I needed to get out. I turned toward the door,

pushing my thoughts into order, trying to plan my next move.

And then a hand caught my wrist.

"You haven't paid for your drink," the bartender said calmly.

My stomach dropped. I turned back; my pulse suddenly too loud in my ears. He wasn't looking at me accusingly. Just…expectantly. Like he already knew. Like he was waiting to see what I would do when I couldn't pay. My SES had fallen to 2.0 after being fired. I was one step above Offload Status. A drink like this—real whiskey, unregulated—wasn't just expensive. It was a privilege. One I no longer had.

I reached for my wristband out of habit, but stopped halfway, fingers curling into a fist. The bartender watched me with quiet amusement. I could already see the outcome. I'd swipe. The scanner would flash red. A warning would ping The Algorithm—"Attempted Unauthorized Purchase." And then? One more drop in score and the drones would appear. I swallowed hard.

"Look, I—"

The bartender waved a hand before I could finish.

"Never mind," he said easily. "This one's on me."

I blinked.

"Say hello to Adam for me," he added, turning away before I could argue.

I opened my mouth, then closed it again. I couldn't pay and he wasn't going to let me if I could. And he wasn't going to answer any more questions. I turned back toward the door, stepping out into the late afternoon light, the tension still thick in my chest. This time I vowed not to hide from Adam. It was high time we met.

I walked for hours. My head finally cleared. Side streets, transit hubs, commercial sectors—everywhere I thought he might be. Nowhere. The city pulsed with the same mechanical efficiency as always. Tram lines flowed overhead, ads adjusted in real-time, security drones hovered lazily above the crowd, scanning wristbands, tracking movements. But Adam was clearly outside of the system. He didn't move like everyone else. Which meant I couldn't find him like everyone else. I had to stop thinking the way I was trained to think. Instead of looking for where he might be—I had to let him show himself.

It was almost by accident then that I saw him. A glimpse — just a flicker of gray — turning into a small storefront between two luxury corporate complexes. "The Second Chapter Bookstore." I barely noticed the name, pushing through the door. A soft chime rang overhead as I stepped inside. The air was cool and quiet. Rows of shelves stretched into the distance, but the place felt almost empty. It was quiet.

Except for the clicking of the wall clock. Just like the one in the bar.

The bookstore owner was dealing with a well-dressed customer at the counter, paying for a book. I saw the SES 4.3 status flash briefly on the transaction screen. Well above mine. Well above safety. I remembered being that safe.

I kept my distance, pretending to browse. I tried

to make out the titles of the books when my head swooned again. *"What's wrong with me"*, I wondered, as my eyes tried to focus. I steadied myself, holdin on to the book case to keep from stumbling. I shook my head and glanced over at the shop owner. She was still busy, and had not noticed me. Or at least she didn't acknowlege me. My body felt like the building was moving. And then the feelings subsided, and I returned to my senses.

I didn't see Adam. He should have been here. I had seen him walk inside. So where—I glanced over to the shopkeeper, but she still ignored me. I guessed that she was all to aware of my 2.1 status. I was too much trouble to help, not enough points to bother with. She'd probably ask me to leave.

The customer finished their transaction and left, the door chime ringing softly behind them. Now, it was just me and the shopkeeper in the store. She was older, maybe in her sixties, dressed simply in a brown cotton dress, hair pulled into a neat bun on the top of her head, with a few soft curls of gray and brown hair poking out. She gave me a soft smile as she took notice of me. I hesitated, knowing that eventually she'd recognize my SES. When she asked if I needed help. I shook my head.

"Just looking." I lied.

She didn't drop the smile. But she also didn't move away. Instead, she studied me for a moment, then—

"Iris," she said gently.

I froze. My name. She had said my name. I hadn't told her.

"Adam is waiting for you," she said.

Every instinct told me to leave. I had been manipulated all day, pushed, led, controlled. But Adam had come here a few moments bfore I had. There is no coincidence in New Columbia, and I didn't know where all this was leading. Maybe to my own offloading? But wasn't I headed there anyway? And if I left now, I might never find him again.

I looked at her with inquisitive eyes. "Where?"

The shopkeeper's hand drifted toward a wall of aged bookshelves, fingers grazing the worn spines with purpose. I watched, puzzled, until she selected a single volume and gave it a gentle pull.

A soft click echoed through the quiet shop.

The entire section of shelving trembled, then shifted. With a low, mechanical groan, the bookcase slid open, revealing a narrow passage shrouded in darkness. The scent of dust and old paper mingled with something else—something colder.

She stepped aside, her expression unreadable, but the slightest hint of amusement flickered in her eyes.

"Go on," she said.

My breath caught in my throat.

Pulse hammering, I stepped forward, into the shadows.

Chapter 7

CAPT. RAYNE GOES HUNTING

Iris Delecroix may be hiding, but she's not going to escape me. I had risen to the rank of Captain within the IBS, not because of any favors, but because I, Evelyn Rayne, knew how to system worked. The Algorithm promised anyone who obeyed and worked hard that they would be rewarded. Failure to do your job meant losing out on those rewards. It was a simple contract. The fact that one Iris Delacroix had eluded me and remained at large was not making me happy. It was not helping my SES either. She was starting to piss me off.

2 P.M. that afternoon I got the notice. She was close. I knew it. The reports had just come in. The Watchers had flagged an anomaly. Iris Delacroix. Her SES had been reported. The Algorithm had caught her, like I trusted it would. Her location: a bookstore on the corner of Aether & 17th. Mid-Tier district. I was already moving before the transmission ended. I weaved through the streets; my enforcer uniform allowed me passage without interference. People stepped aside, even stepping into the street to avoid delaying an officer of the people. The city was waking

up—workers moving in coordinated patterns, traffic streams flowing in perfect synchronization. All of them showing deference to me, an Enforcer on duty.

Screens along the walkways projected the morning reports, replaying Callus' latest address.

"We are closer than ever to a truly perfected state. Deviance has reached its lowest levels in recorded history.
The Algorithm sees all. And it does not err."

It does not err. I repeated the words in my head like a mantra. The Algorithm had identified Iris. And now I had her.

When I arrived at the bookstore, the drones were floating nearby, ensuring that she was still inside. The place was quiet. Small. Unremarkable. The kind of shop people wandered into for nostalgia, not necessity. Paper books. Obsolete. Sentimental.

I despised places like this. Books were dangerous. Paper books were the last vestiges of an era where truth had been subjective, where anyone could write, publish, and distribute lies without oversight. Before the Algorithm, before optimization, before Callus, people had been allowed to indulge in fantasy, delusion, poison—and they called it education.

And children—fragile, susceptible children—had been their primary victims. I remembered the first time I saw a banned book at the Academy. I was fourteen. It was part of an exercise—controlled exposure, designed to show us the dangers of ideological corruption. I had turned the pages carefully, almost reverently, because even then I understood that this was not to be trifled with. I was handling something... dangerous.

"All people deserve freedom ... Freedom is the ability to decide for oneself ... A society thrives on freedom, compassion and charity."

I remember the instructor watching me, waiting. I remember the way my hands tightened on the pages, the growing, gnawing feeling inside me that something about these words was wrong. The instructor nodded. "You understand, don't you?" she had said. "You feel the weakness in the words."

I did.

Before Callus, words had infected everything. They had warped minds, twisted perceptions, made people believe they could redefine reality just by claiming it was so. Men could be women. Women could be men. Sex was a spectrum. Marriage had no meaning. Nations could function without hierarchy, without order, without rules. Lies. And lies were contagious. How many children had read some old-world fantasy of rebellion, believing themselves heroes against imagined tyranny? How many had turned against the system because a book had made them think authority was the enemy?

There was a time when people encouraged this. Let them read, they had said. Let them explore ideas. And where had that led? Chaos. Collapse. Society had drowned in its own contradictions, strangled by the very "freedoms" it had claimed to uphold. But Callus had fixed that. He had understood that the truth was not something to be debated. Truth was something to be defined.

The old books had been purged, their digital counterparts rewritten and corrected. The Algorithm ensured that history was recorded properly, without the errors of human bias. And yet, places like this still existed.

I stepped inside. The door chimed softly behind me, a delicate sound swallowed by the heavy quiet of the shop. The air was thick—dust, old paper, something faintly metallic just beneath it. Warm light pooled in low halos, casting long shadows between the shelves. A mechanical clock ticked somewhere in the background, slow and deliberate, measuring out time like a heartbeat.

I took a step forward, then hesitated. A strange weight pressed at the edges of my perception, a momentary unsteadiness. The sensation passed as quickly as it came, leaving behind a vague sense of disorientation. I exhaled, steadying myself. Maybe it was the close air, the dim lighting. Maybe it was nothing at all. But for half a second, I felt like I had missed a step in a staircase I hadn't known was there. A woman stood behind the counter, middle-aged, with tired eyes and the kind of wary posture that told me she already knew who I was. I approached slowly.

"Good morning." My voice was even, polite. No need for force. Yet.

The shopkeeper smiled back. "Good morning, Officer. How can I help you?"

I studied her. She was calm, confident, a little too

sure of herself, I thought.

"I'm looking for someone."

She did not react.

"A woman," I continued. "Mid-thirties. Dark hair. Last seen wearing a gray coat. She was here yesterday evening." I stepped closer, lowering my voice.

"I'm not asking if you saw her. I already know she was here. I'm asking where she went."

The shopkeeper's eyes never left mine. "I had several customers yesterday ..."

The arrogance appalled me. How dare she act like she didn't know. I stopped her mid-sentence.

"A woman is known to have come into your store and there is no record of her leaving," I glared. "I think you would have noticed that."

The woman still did not flinch. "I'm afraid I can't help you. As you can see, there's no-one here but myself. Perhaps the record didn't see her. Sometimes we don't always see what we think we see."

I reached into my coat, activating my terminal with a flick of my wrist. The holo-display flared to life, showing her SES profile. 3.1. Barely above the good standing line. I entered a command. The number plummeted. 3.1 → 2.9. Her wrist monitor blinked red.

"Would you like to reconsider? I asked her.

She looked up at me. There was no expression in her face, as if it wasn't registering what I had done. She should have known full well what this meant. SES 2.9 wasn't fatal. Not yet. But it was dangerous. It meant restricted access. Higher surveillance. If she dropped lower, it meant no health care. No city privileges. No job. It meant the threat of offloading.

I leaned in slightly. "Last chance. Where did she go?"

The shopkeeper's body language remained oddly calm. She did not flinch.

"I told you. I don't know."

I stepped back, exhaling slowly. No visible exits. No trace. That meant there was a back route I couldn't see. The resistance had grown smarter—but not smarter than me. I tapped my terminal again.

"Request LIDAR sweep: Building ID #3827A."

A confirmation pinged back immediately. Drones dispatched. Within the hour, the building would be mapped in full—every hidden compartment, every tunnel, every crack. Nothing could be concealed. Marion's words from yesterday echoed in my mind.

"We're close now. Another few cycles, and we'll have full compliance."

Yes. We were.

I took one last look at the shopkeeper. She hadn't moved but her eyes showed no fear ... only hatred. Without another word, I turned and walked out. It would take some time for the LIDAR reports to be complete, so I would just have to wait. A lesser mind might have questioned how a single woman like Iris could evade the Algorithm for this long. But I knew the truth. The Algorithm was processing. It was learning. And when it adapted, when it saw through her deception, she would have nowhere left to run.

She thinks she's free. But not for long.

As I turned to leave I once again I suddenly felt

unsteady on my feet. Old buildings like this were a nightmare. I clenched my jaw, forcing my stride to steady, unwilling to let the woman behind the counter see even a flicker of weakness on my part. I walked out, shaking off the lingering unease as I stepped back into the world I understood.

Chapter 8

IRIS MEETS ADAM

Once I had slipped through the hidden passage inside the bookstore, I followed the faint glow of overhead lights, my steps cautious as the narrow corridor guided me toward an open door.

He was waiting. Older than I expected—late forties, maybe early fifties. Salt-and-pepper hair, neatly cut. Gray eyes, sharp and unreadable. He stood with easy confidence, his posture steady, deliberate. There was something refined about him—educated, calculated. He wore a gray sports jacket over a crisp blue oxford shirt, the kind of effortless style that spoke of someone who had once moved in important circles. He wasn't bulky, but fit, like someone who kept himself in shape without vanity.

As I crossed the threshold, his eyes locked onto mine, sharp and assessing—like he was bracing for me to turn and run. He wasn't wrong. Every instinct screamed at me to do exactly that. I had just followed him into the bookstore. Stepped through a concealed doorway. And now, I stood in a dimly lit back room, face to face with the man who had been stalking me for days. And yet, I wasn't afraid. I was curious.

He set down his drink and stood to greet me. The

cut crystal tumbler looked very much like the ones the bartender had been polishing so carefully.

"Hello Iris," he said carefully.

I stared, squinting my eyes. "You know my name."

A flicker of amusement crossed his face. "I do."

I waited for an explanation. It didn't come. Instead, he tilted his head slightly.

"Do you want to sit?"

I glanced at the worn-out chair in the corner but stayed standing. He nodded like he expected that.

"Alright," he said. "First off, I owe you an apology."

That threw me.

"An apology?" I repeated.

"For frightening you," he said. "I had to be sure you were who I thought you were."

"And who, exactly, do you think I am?"

His expression darkened.

"A woman who recently made herself very dangerous."

I exhaled slowly, keeping my voice even.

"OK," I started, "Let's begin with something simple," I looked at him with as much courage as I could muster. "Who the hell are you?"

Adam body language shifted, relaxed, he let his arms drop a little. "I'm sorry, how rude of me. I should have led with that. My name is Adam Solace."

I swallowed, keeping my expression neutral, but inside, my mind raced. He was watching me closely, waiting for my reaction. I had not wanted to give him one but the blood rushing to my face couldn't be denied.

"You say that... like it's supposed to mean something to me," I said evenly, pretending I didn't recognize him."

He grinned. "Oh, I think it does."

I forced a hollow laugh. "Why would I know you?"

"Because you have pretended to be me."

Silence. For a split second, my breath caught. But I recovered quickly. I didn't deny it. Didn't confirm it either. Adam waited, studying me like I was a puzzle he had almost—but not quite—solved.

"I don't know what you're talking about," I lied.

"Don't you?" His voice was mild, but there was something sharper beneath it. "Someone broke into the system using security access belonging to an erased man. A ghost. A digital corpse." He tapped his temple. "And I happen to be very familiar with ghosts."

I crossed my arms defensively. Was that a threat? The room felt smaller now. He still didn't feel threatening, exactly. My mind flickered back to that night—the glow of the secure terminal, the whir of the processors, the way my fingers had hovered over the keys as I had entered the name: Adam Solace. At the time, I hadn't questioned it. His credentials had been perfect. A 6.1 SES clearance, unrestricted access. No flagged behaviors, no security locks. Clean. But there had been something else. Something wrong. A second score. It had flashed on the screen for just a second— then disappeared. I should have stopped there. Should have wondered why a single name had two SES scores. Instead, I had used it to break into the system. And now, here I was. Face to face with the man I had unknowingly stolen from.

Still, I kept my voice steady. "If someone broke into the system, what makes you assume it was me?"

Adam's sighed. "I don't assume."

I swallowed hard.

"So, you broke into my apartment looking for the files?"

"I did."

"And tore my place apart for them?"

He sighed. "No. That wasn't me."

I narrowed my eyes. "Right. Just a coincidence that my place was ransacked the same night you decided to pay a visit?"

"Hollis and the enforcers were coming for you. I wanted to get there before them."

I tilted my head.

A slow, tense silence settled between us. I shifted slightly, feeling the small drive in my pocket. Hollis had known about the files. Who else did? They'd gotten me fired, flagged for offloading, and threatened to be erased from New Columbia's system.

I knew the risk the moment I started my investigation. I had built my life on chasing hidden truths, exposing the lies that held this city together. I knew how dangerous the truth was, and I wasn't about to leave files laying around. No one stood a chance of finding anything. But I didn't say that. Instead, I pressed on, trying to see how much he knew.

"And what did you find?"

He hesitated. "I found nothing."

His expression darkened. "I am hoping you'll

be open to working with me. The files you have are crucial to my work," he said. "And right now, they are crucial to your survival."

His eyes met mine and held. Dark gray eyes, set into a soft but serious face. His eyes scared me a little, or maybe excited me. I looked away.

His gaze at me remained steady. "Iris, if they get a hold of that file, we are both going to be in grave danger."

"You still have a choice," he added.

I let out a breath, steady but slow. "A choice," I repeated. "You mean the part where I decide whether to trust you or trust the system?"

He slowly nodded his head, his lips tightened against his teeth. Not quite a smile.

"Exactly."

I unfolded my arms. "And if I just walk out of here?"

"You won't get far." His voice was quiet, his statement an undeniable fact. "The enforcers flagged you. You're already bleeding out of the system. A few more days, maybe minutes, and you'll be offloaded." He paused. "Or worse—Recalibrated"

The word hung between us, heavy with all the stories I'd heard but never been allowed to print. Some people got second chances. Only to come back... not quite right, wrong in fact. "Recalibrated"

I exhaled sharply. "What exactly are you offering me, Adam?"

His eyes gleamed. "Let me tell you a story," he said.

"Six years ago," he said, "I was offloaded."

I raised my eyebrows. "And yet, here you are. Walking around the streets, witnessing other people being offloaded. Commenting to strange--" I stopped myself short realizing we hadn't been strangers. "Anyway, how do you survive offloading?"

"Because by the time the drones took me to the Undercity—I didn't exist anymore."

I frowned. "That's not how Offloading works. You don't just—" I stopped. "Wait. Someone erased you first?"

His eyes flickered with something close to amusement. "Now you're getting it."

I shook my head, trying to process. "That's not possible. The system logs every SES drop in real-time. The moment someone hits 1.9, they're immediately flagged for processing."

"Exactly," Adam said. "That's what happens when the system can see you."

Something cold settled in my stomach.

"And it didn't see you?"

"It did" he replied, "I never hit 1.9"

I stared at him. "You're telling me you figured out how to override the SES scoring?"

"Sort of. I put an Easter egg in the system to delete myself the moment I hit 1.99999. A safety measure." He shrugged. "I worked in system security. I had access. I learned how The Algorithm processed identities— how it stored, tracked, and erased people when their SES dropped too low. And I thought it might come in handy someday. As you can see, it did."

I narrowed my eyes. "What kind of Easter egg?"

"A code-skip to Final Asset Processing," he said simply.

"Final Asset Processing is an internal command," I said. "It's the last step in Offloading. The moment it's executed, a person is wiped from the system completely—no record, no recovery. They're unrecoverable data."

Adam nodded. "Exactly."

I shook my head. "It's the final code in offloading proceedure."

He smiled slightly. "Unless you command it to run it first."

I finally put two and two together.

"You ran it backwards; That would mean it offloaded a non-entity?" I asked slowly.

He nodded.

"And when the drones came for you…"

"The system didn't recognize me." He spread his hands. "As far as it was concerned, I wasn't there at all."

I let out a slow, stunned breath. "But why would they even take you if you were erased?"

"Even though my record was gone, the enforcer drones had instructions to retrieve someone. The system has a fail-safe for unexpected cases. When an SES-linked citizen is flagged for offloading, but their records are missing or corrupted, the drones default to bio-metric tracking. I still had a body. A location. A presence. The Algorithm treated me as an unclassified entity."

"Meaning what?" I asked.

"Treated me like an offloaded and processed me anyway. This was an error correction protocol. The system couldn't explain what I was—so it categorized me as a lost asset and dumped me into the Undercity without full processing."

"And what happened when they dropped you off in the Undercity?"

Adam's expression darkened.

"That's when I learned the truth."

Adam leaned against the desk, his voice lower now.

"You ever wonder why no one ever breaks out of the Undercity?" he asked.

I scoffed. "That's easy. No SES ensures no access to the city. No food. No shelter. They're locked out of the system entirely, nothing to go back to."

"That's a logical reason," Adam said. "But that's not why they stay."

Something about his tone sent a chill down my spine.

I hesitated. "Then why?"

Adam met my gaze.

"Because The Algorithm keeps them there."

I frowned. "You mean physical barriers?"

"No," he said. "I mean their minds."

A sick feeling curled in my gut.

"What are you saying?" I asked, my voice quieter now.

Adam exhaled. "The Undercity isn't just a slum,

Iris. It's a cognitive prison. A cage built inside their own heads."

I shook my head. "That's not—"

"Every offloaded citizen is connected to the system the moment they arrive," he interrupted. "Neurologically. The Algorithm rewires their perception. It traps them in a closed loop of suffering. No matter how far they run, they always find themselves back where they started. The perfect prison, with no walls, no guards—just control."

"That's insanity."

"And it's efficient," Adam countered. "No fences. No tracking devices. Just an invisible leash that keeps them from ever realizing they could leave."

I tried to push back. "If that were true, surely someone could have figured it out. Someone would have escaped—"

Adam gave me a sharp look. "They don't. Because The Algorithm doesn't just trap them—it erases the idea of escape from their minds."

I stiffened.

"The ones who start questioning things?" he continued. "The ones who try to leave? They start forgetting. Losing time. Thought fragments. The Algorithm redirects their perception, makes them think they never tried in the first place. Eventually… they stop trying at all."

The room felt colder.

I could picture it—millions of discarded people, living in loops, retracing their own steps, unable to remember that they had walked this same path before.

Trapped in an endless, shifting maze with no exits, no hope.

I wet my lips. "And you?" I asked. "Why didn't it work on you?"

Adam's expression was grim.

"Because when I stepped through those gates," he said, "The Algorithm didn't see me. They took my body. But they never processed my mind. The final process is neurological control. Once that's complete the system can report "Final Processing Complete, and in my case, it thought it had."

I exhaled slowly, trying to process what he was saying. "You said you weren't the only one."

"I wasn't."

Adam leaned against the desk, his voice calm but deliberate.

"When I first stepped into the Undercity, I thought I was done," he said. "That was supposed to be the end of me—processed, erased, forgotten. But instead, I woke up."

I watched him carefully, unsure where this was going.

"The Algorithm never finished the job," he continued. "It took my body. But it didn't go further."

I swallowed. "You knew you weren't trapped"

Adam nodded.

"As far as the system was concerned, I am a ghost. I slipped back into New Columbia. I found some people I trusted—people I needed who like me, were on a downward path towards 1.9. And I erased them before the system could."

My breath caught.

I shook my head, struggling to wrap my mind around it.

"You built a network of ghosts," I said slowly.

Adam chose his words carefully. "Not all at once. It had to be gradual. Only a few of us, since we can't tip off the system. Too many unexplained disappearances would have triggered system alerts. But a few isolated cases? The Algorithm doesn't waste the CPU energy resources. We fell into the category of 'acceptable statistical deviation'."

"Without digital identities, how could you get back into New Columbia? The drones would have surely noticed you and classified you as an illegal alien the moment you stepped onto the street."

Adam beamed. "You're absolutely right. I took advantage of another statistic. Every year, tens of thousands of people move up and down in their SES status, shifting downward due to unpaid debts, infractions, or flagged behaviors or moving up by hitting merit tests and social skills. Many of these people hover on the verge of offloading, but the system predicts that they will struggle hard enough to avoid the last drop to offloading."

"You just described 80 percent of the people of New Columbia'" I sighed. "But why not give yourselves some power? Jump right in as a 6.0?

"Precisely because we want to be in that 80%! As you know, the SES system prioritizes efficiency. High-status citizens like that are constantly monitored, their spending patterns scrutinized, their every movement tracked. One, because there are less of them to monitor, and two—they are assumed to be at higher risk of significant corruption. But mid-to-low-tier citizens? The system expects them to struggle. It assumes that people with SES between 2.8 and 3.5 are statistically in the middle of the bell curve—unimportant, and ultimately irrelevant. That makes it easier for my team to insert us as mid-tier citizens since these people are for the most part - unremarkable.

"You used the Algorithm's own bias against the common person!"

"Right again! My tech specialists hacked transit logs, employment databases, and housing assignments, ensuring that their new identities had a believable history of financial setbacks, lost promotions, or minor infractions. These artificial records reflected people who had fallen in rank but were still part of the system, so when seen by a drone, it takes a quick look at our status and recent histories, deems us unremarkable and goes back to looking for bigger fish."

"And the people who have already been offloaded? Can they be helped" I asked, already knowing the answer.

Adam's enthusiasm faded.

"For them, it is too late," he said quietly. "Their minds had already been rewritten. Even if we could pull them out, they wouldn't be themselves anymore. The human mind isn't a computer. When the neurons have been rewired, that person is lost. Every day we watch the more and more being deposited.."

I swallowed the tightness in my throat.

"You stopped trying," I said.

He nodded. "It's too late for them. They aren't dead, but I think I would rather be. And what's worse, we have found that most don't want to be saved. I have offered to help people I knew I could use, only to have them tell me I was crazy and that they trusted the system to keep them safe. It rarely if ever does."

I felt something shift inside me.

A part of me had always known—always suspected—that the system was more than just control. That it was rewriting reality, shaping the thinking of the citizens it was supposedly there to protect. But hearing it confirmed made my stomach churn. Adam pushed off the desk and stepped closer.

"Iris," he said, voice lower now. "Right now, you have a choice. You can fight to get back into a system that wants you dead. Or you can disappear. But only if you join us. I can't force you to turn over your files, but right now it is your only ticket out. I am offering."

I tensed. "Just like that?"

"Just like that," he said. "The moment we erase you, The Algorithm won't be able to track you. You'll be free to move without a digital footprint. No more SES scores. No more surveillance. No more fear."

A hollow laugh escaped me. "And all I have to do is give you my file?"

Adam's wry smile returned. "It's a fair trade, don't you think?"

I hesitated.

"We call ourselves the Ghosts in the Republic.

I swallowed. "How many of you are there?"

"Not enough," he said simply.

He tilted his head slightly. "Don't you want a way out of your predicament, Iris?"

He stepped forward, closing the space between us. He didn't touch me, didn't reach for me, but his presence carried weight. A gravity I wasn't sure I wanted to fight.

"Iris, you've spent your life chasing truth. But the truth inside New Columbia is a lie, wrapped in another lie, buried under a thousand more. If you really want to see what's underneath, you must be willing to let go of the person the system says you are."

I hesitated. "And if I do?"

"Then you'll see what I see. The world behind the world."

I swallowed. "The Ghost Network."

Adam nodded. "But only if you're ready."

I looked past him; I had spent years peeling back layers of deception, and now, I was standing at the edge of something even deeper. Erase myself or be erased. Some choice. But I already knew my answer. It was just a matter of who did the erasing.

I met his gaze. "Do it."

Something flickered across Adam's face— approval, maybe. Or relief. He reached into his coat, pulled out a small black device, and placed it on the table between us. A slim interface, flat and curved, designed to fit the curve of my arm.

"You're ready?" he asked, one last time.

I wasn't. But I nodded anyway. Adam pressed

his thumb to the unit and held it to my wrist. The lights of my SES flickered. The system accessed my identity, processed my existence. And then, in less than a second— my screen went black. then the words flashed and disappeared

"FINAL ASSET PROCESS COMPLETE."

I had expected something to feel different. Some seismic shift, some sudden, terrifying sense of emptiness. But there was only silence. A strange, unsettling quiet in my chest, like a tether had been cut that I hadn't even realized was there. Adam watched me, waiting for the moment it hit.

"You feel it yet?" he asked.

I swallowed. "I don't know what I feel."

He laughed, as if that was the right answer. "Exactly there's no difference, except now, the Algorithm can't see you."

"Hey!" I said suddenly remembering another of his little magic tricks, "one more thing I need to know."

Adam looked at me expectantly.

"How the hell were you following me up there? Every time I turned around, there you were."

Adam smiled. "Was I?"

"Every time I turned a corner; you were already waiting for me. I switched streets, doubled back, cut through crowds. It didn't matter. You were always one step ahead of me. How could you anticipate where I was going? It was like you were cloned."

"And you're sure it was me?" He winked.

I narrowed my eyes, turning my head slightly.

"Remember our discussion about how the offloaded never tried to escape the Undercity? When I told you the Algorithm redirects their perceptions—makes them think they can't leave? '

"Yes, so?" I hesitated, wondering where this was going.

"You only thought you saw me."

I stared at Adam, mouth open.

"It's an old hypnotist's trick. The human brain is wired for pattern recognition, right? It fills in blanks, makes assumptions to save time. I used the Algorithm project an image…nudge you along. You never saw me; you only caught glimpses of a hologram."

"You were herding me."

Adam smiled. It was his next statement that floored me.

"I needed you to be where I could talk to you. Only the bar and the bookstore are equipped with special equipment to cloak appearances. That's why you didn't recognize me as the bartender. Did you?"

He raised his drink and winked. "Or even the bookstore owner."

I stood motionless, my jaw dropped open. I couldn't find the words to respond. He continued.

"Tell me Iris, what is the first thing you remember about the bar and the bookstore? First thing that comes to mind?" he asked.

I frowned, searching my memory. I remember entering the building and the sound... the sound of...

"The clock." I said suddenly. Both had old-fashioned wind-up wall clocks. I immediately remembered the loud ticking.

Adam's smile widened. "Exactly."

I blinked. "What does that have to do with—?"

"You heard it the moment you walked in, didn't you?" He leaned forward, setting his drink down. "That steady, rhythmic tick. Not digital. Not synthetic. A real, mechanical clock. Your brain noticed it before anything else."

I hesitated. "I guess so."

Adam nodded. "That's because it wasn't just a clock. It was the anchor."

"The anchor for what?"

"For your perception." He sat back, watching me carefully. "Just like the Algorithm, the human brain isn't a perfect recorder, Iris. It doesn't capture reality—it interprets it. It fills in gaps, adjusts for context, smooths over inconsistencies so you don't even notice. Now, what if someone could... nudge those adjustments? Redirect those interpretations?"

A chill prickled down my spine. "You're saying you... altered my perception?"

"Not directly." He gestured vaguely, as if reaching for the right words. "I just introduced a variable. A little... temporal drift."

I narrowed my eyes. "What the hell does that mean?"

He gave me a fatherly smile. It was tender and warm.

"You ever lose track of time, Iris? Walk into a

room and suddenly forget why you're there? Have a conversation and later remember details just slightly off from how they happened?"

I nodded warily.

"That's your brain compensating for minor disruptions in perception. It happens all the time. The clock—well, let's just say it helps that process along." He picked up his drink again, swirling the amber liquid. "It disorients your temporal awareness just enough that your mind starts making little... corrections. And those corrections? That's where I slip in."

I stared at him, remembering the echo of that clock in my head. As if I could still hear them. A constant metronome.

"You saw as a bartender, because you expected to see a bartender. Your brain filled in the details— something more expected, more reasonable. A safe person. An unimportant detail."

I shook my head. "No, wait. I talked to you. I looked right at you."

"You talked to someone," he corrected. "And by the time you left, you had already forgotten what he looked like. Tell me. Can you describe him?"

I shot him a look of dismissal. "Of course I can, he was..." My mind drew a blank. When I tried to conjure his face in my mind, there was nothing there. No indelible memory, no characteristics I could draw from. It was just a few hours ago!

He smiled. "Voila"

Suddenly he changed the topic.

Come on," he said, heading toward the back of the room. "There's something I want to show you."

I followed. He led me through a narrow passage, down a flight of metal stairs that creaked under our weight. The air changed as we descended—colder, thicker, tinged with something electric. I felt it in my skin, in my teeth, in the back of my skull. We stepped through a rusted doorway. And suddenly, the world dropped away.

I froze as we stepped out onto the fire escape high above the city, a city that shouldn't exist. Towers of scavenged neon, bridges made of repurposed steel, screens flickering with stolen light. People moved like currents, slipping through the shadows, faces half-lit by the glow of underground terminals. The whisper of machinery filled the air—The Undercity. Not just slums. Not just ruins. A second world. Hidden. Thriving. Adam turned to me, watching my reaction.

"Welcome to the other side," he said. "Welcome to the Ghost Network."

Chapter 9

IRIS IN THE UNDERCITY

The Undercity was nothing like I had imagined. I had spent years writing about it, shaping its image for the people of New Columbia through carefully approved narratives. The stories were always the same—a cautionary tale, a necessary evil, the last stop for those who had failed the social contract. But now, walking through its winding corridors, I realized how little I had understood.

There were no screaming masses, no wild lawlessness, no feral offloaded tearing at each other in desperation. There was order. Unspoken, unseen—but order nonetheless. Adam walked beside me, hands in his coat pockets, leading me through the maze of passageways that made up the Ghost-controlled sectors. I tried not to stare at the people we passed. Not all of them were broken. Some were watchful, moving with quiet purpose. The Ghosts, I realized. Those who had seen through the illusion.

"I expected worse," I admitted, breaking the silence.

Adam grinned. "That's by design. New Columbia needs people to believe this place is a hellhole. Keeps them obedient."

"I spent my career feeding that lie."

"Not just you," he said. "Everyone does. That's how the system works. People think they're shaping the truth when all they're doing is repeating what's been shaped for them."

A bitter laugh escaped me. "That's the sort of comment that would have gotten me offloaded."

Adam gave me a sideways glance. "That, and trusting the wrong people."

I frowned. "You mean Hollis."

He nodded.

I hesitated before speaking. "I don't think he wanted to betray me."

Adam snorted. "No?"

I sighed. "He said he fought for me."

The passage narrowed as we turned a corner, leading into an open-air section of the underground—a collapsed transit hub, its ceiling cracked open just enough for pale, artificial daylight to seep through. The sight was surreal. The remnants of old train platforms were now makeshift homes, the steel framework above tangled with vines that had fought their way through concrete. It should have looked ruined. Instead, it looked... I don't know. . . lived in.

I stopped to take it in. "I don't understand why he turned me in."

Adam leaned against a rusted pillar, watching me carefully. "I do."

I met his gaze. "Then tell me."

He ran a hand through his thick silvery hair. "You already knew The Truth was state-controlled. But you still thought you could push the boundaries. That you could plant the right ideas in just the right way."

I bristled. "I didn't think. I knew. Callus doesn't tolerate direct defiance, but he's paranoid. The moment he suspects his own people of working against him, he won't stop until he's rooted them out. I wasn't trying to start a revolution. I was trying to make the ones at the top tear each other apart."

Adam studied me. "Smart. Risky as hell. But smart."

I turned to face him full on. "It would have worked. If Hollis hadn't turned me in."

Adam met my eyes, then looked down. "Would it have?"

I narrowed my eyes. "You think it wouldn't?"

"I think," Adam said, "that you underestimated how fragile people like Hollis really are, or how precariously positioned you were."

I frowned, waiting for him to explain.

He shifted his eyes, following the flight of a pigeon as it flew towards an opening in the broken glass ceiling high above us. We were standing in what was once a domed underground train terminal. Light from the city bled through the grit-stained and yellowed glass. The bird flew up and out of the opening, followed by another. Unlike all the poor souls down here, they still had the freedom to come and go.

"Hollis didn't betray you out of malice. He did it out of fear."

I scoffed. "Fear of what? He's spent years molding The Truth into a propaganda machine. He knew exactly what he was doing."

"That's just it," Adam said. "He knew exactly what he was doing—and he knew exactly how easily he could be replaced. Hollis knew he wasn't special. He was just a useful tool. And the second The Board started looking at you, he knew what it meant."

I suddenly felt like I was standing on the edge of something vast, something I couldn't see the bottom of. "They were watching me before he said anything, weren't they?"

Adam nodded. "They watch everyone. Hollis was just the confirmation they needed."

My mind stalled, caught between disbelief and inevitability. I let out a slow breath, glancing around the ruins of the old transit hub. I had spent so much time digging through lies, chasing the threads of corruption, uncovering how the system worked. Carefully covering my tracks from the watchful eyes of the observers, the enforcers and the algorithm. But in the end, it hadn't been The Algorithm, the Board, or even the Enforcers that had brought me down.

It had been a man afraid of losing his position.

"It wasn't just them that noticed your actions. I saw it as well," he said.

His words left me standing in a world I no longer recognized.

Adam and I walked deeper into the Undercity, past the remnants of a world that no longer existed. Crumbling infrastructure, old transit tunnels turned into makeshift shelters, the bones of a civilization that had been erased—just like me. I should have been afraid. I should have felt lost. But instead, I felt something close to relief. For the first time in my life, I was outside the system. No SES. No Algorithm tracking my every move. No scripted narratives shaping my reality. Just me, the man walking beside me, and the truth I was still trying to piece together. Finally I glanced over at Adam.

"Hollis told me you were watching me too. Well, he showed me the photos with you in them."

He nodded. "That's right."

"Why?"

He pointed at his own face, letting his finger slowly trace circles. "I built half the security protocols you broke into, Iris. Did you really think I wouldn't notice?"

"Why didn't you approach me then?"

"Because I wanted to see what you were after." He shot me a sideways glance. "And once I found out, I knew you were either going to be the dumbest person in New Columbia... or the most dangerous."

I huffed. "And which is it?"

He grinned. "Still deciding."

My mind wandered back to our discussion about Hollis. I still had so many questions about them I thought I knew.

"What else do you know about Hollis. Why did he show me the file if he wanted to throw me under the bus? Why did he tell me to run?"

Adam's grin faded. "Because he was weak. He didn't turn you in because he thought you were doing something wrong. He did it because he thought it would save him. He probably showed you the files to appease his own conscious."

I watched Adam as he carefully picked his path over the uneven broken concrete of the sidewalk, occasionally taking my arm to step across the wider gaps.

"Hollis built his entire career on playing it safe. On knowing exactly where the line was and making sure he never stepped over it. He wasn't ambitious— he didn't want real power. He just wanted to keep his position, keep his comfort, and not end up like the people he threw under the bus."

I had to agree. It made sense. Too much sense.

"So when The Board started watching me," I said slowly, "he saw his opportunity for some brownie-points."

Adam nodded. "You were becoming a liability. And liabilities get offloaded. If he stayed quiet, they'd start wondering about his loyalties. They could accuse him of covering up, questioning how long he'd known. He started gathering the info in the file he showed you. Building a case against you."

"He actually planned to sell me out to prove his loyalty?"

Adam shook his head dismissively. "Yet it still wasn't enough."

I frowned. "What do you mean?"

"He thought he was buying himself safety," Adam said. "Instead, he just proved what they already suspected."

I hesitated. "Which was?"

"That he was undependable."

A heavy silence settled between us.

I exhaled, shaking my head. "Do you know what happened?"

Adam nodded. "Three Oligarchs. No warning, no formality. Just a quiet little meeting where they told him he was on probation."

I blinked. "Probation? For what?"

"For being weak," Adam corrected. "The Board doesn't reward loyalty. They reward strength. And Hollis? He showed them he was the kind of man who would betray his own people just to save himself."

Every word, every promise, replayed in my mind, now hollow and sharp.

"What happens to him now?"

Adam shrugged. "Who knows? Maybe he clings on a little longer. Maybe they offload him in a month. Maybe he finds a way to convince the Oligarchs that he's not a liability."

I let that sink in, the truth hitting me all at once.

"Or maybe he tries to fix his mistake."

Adam's gaze was steady. "Right. People like Hollis don't get second chances. He knows that. He also knows The Board will need one last use for him before they cut him loose."

Understanding snapped into place, sharp and unavoidable.

"He was the one who trashed my apartment."

Adam nodded. "If he can get his hands on your files, he has a bargaining chip with them."

A quiet urgency built inside me, insistent and

unwelcome.

"Turning you in the first time only delayed his downfall. The only way to prove his loyalty now is to finish the job."

I felt my fingers tighten into fists. I had spent weeks trying to stay one step ahead of The Board, the Enforcers, and the damn Algorithm itself. The thought of Hollis hunting me down left me feeling caught between disbelief and inevitability.

"Hollis isn't your biggest threat," Adam cut in.

I turned to him sharply. "What do you mean?"

Adam sighed, raking a hand through his hair. "There's someone else who wants you just as badly, more perhaps."

"Who?"

"Evelyn Rayne."

"She can't find me and its killing her," I murmured.

Adam nodded. " Enforcers can't fail. It's just not an option for them."

Chapter 10

THE INTERVIEW WITH CALLUS

As we walked through the Undercity, Adam quizzed me on my background.

"You know, I haven't always been a reporter on the run," I told him.

"I am well aware," he replied, adding "I watched your interview with Callus."

I cringed. He noticed.

"I take it there's more to the story."

"It pretty much is the reason I am here right now" I agreed. "Now its my turn to tell you a story."

The invitation had arrived in a black envelope, sealed with the golden insignia of the Chancellor's office. At first, I thought it was a mistake. Or a test. Or a trap. Because Orin Callus didn't give interviews. Not real ones. Not unscripted. The Truth—New Columbia's only state-approved news source—had long since perfected the art of manufacturing his voice. His speeches were edited, filtered through The Algorithm, reworked into something flawless, indisputable, absolute. He didn't need journalists.

So why me?

At the time, I told myself it was a reward. A recognition of my status, my loyalty, my years of careful reporting. I had spent my career walking the line, asking the right questions but never the wrong ones, peeling back layers just enough to expose minor, acceptable scandals while keeping the deeper rot untouched. I was trusted. Respected. And now, I had been chosen. The exclusive first-person interview with Orin Callus. This was the crown jewel of my career, the piece that would cement me as the top journalist in New Columbia. Even Hollis had been impressed.

"Don't screw this up, Delacroix," he had muttered, sliding the invitation across my desk. "You're the first to sit with him in over a decade."

I wouldn't screw it up. I had spent weeks preparing, crafting the perfect list of questions. I imagined an intellectual sparring match—Callus, the visionary architect of modern society, sharing his philosophies, his strategies for governance. I envisioned a glimpse into the mind of the man who had rebuilt the world. I was prepared to be awed. Instead, I found a rambling, paranoid old man with a powdered face and a comb-over that wouldn't stay in place. Instead, I found a mad king. And by the time I walked out of that room, I knew: This wasn't the greatest moment of my career. It was the beginning of its end.

Callus looked worse in person than he did on TV.

His official portraits were carefully retouched, airbrushed to give the illusion of vitality, but sitting across from him now, I could see the truth. His skin sagged, loose jowls pulling at the corners of his mouth, his circulation poor, leaving a strange blotchy redness along his neck and the backs of his hands. His fingers were thick and swollen, his nails ridged, his knuckles yellowed from too much artificial sweetener, too little real nutrition. But the most unsettling part was his face.

His cheeks were powdered too thickly, the tone mismatched against his forehead, giving him a strange, almost theatrical appearance. His foundation settled into the deep creases around his mouth, making them look deeper, more grotesque. His eyebrows were penciled in too darkly, and the contrast against his thinning, wispy comb-over made him look like a badly aged stage actor—one who refused to leave the spotlight. Yet when he spoke, I almost forgot all of it. Because Callus knew how to speak. His voice carried an undeniable gravity, every phrase delivered with absolute authority, no matter how absurd.

I was here for an exclusive interview—a reward for my loyalty. A chance to sit with the great Orin Callus, the man who had saved New Columbia, the man who had built the perfect society. I had come prepared with sharp, intelligent questions about policy, governance, and the future of the city. I should have known better.

"Miss Delacroix," he said, adjusting his too-tight collar, his fingers leaving smudges of powder on the stiff fabric. "Do you know what makes a society great?"

I kept my expression neutral. "Strength?"

He nodded approvingly. "That's what they all say. Strength. Order. Power. But no—loyalty. That's the real foundation. People don't need freedom. They don't need choices. They need to believe."

I gave the expected nod. "Of course, Chancellor.

Loyalty to the Algorithm ensures—"

He waved his pudgy fingers dismissively. "The Algorithm, sure. Yes, yes. But loyalty to me, first and foremost. People don't love a machine, Miss Delacroix. They need a leader. Someone to guide them. Someone to tell them what's real."

He leaned forward slightly, his stomach pressing into the desk, his comb-over slipping out of place. He fixed it with a quick, greasy swipe.

"You don't know this, but…" he lowered his voice, his tone conspiratorial, "the first leaders didn't even have machines to help them. Can you imagine? Just people, trying to figure things out on their own. It's a wonder civilization survived at all."

I nodded again, keeping my polite smile frozen in place. This was fine. This was still usable. And then the crazy began.

"You'll be as surprised to learn as I was," he continued, "that the real threat to our nation isn't just weak governance. No, no, no. You see, a lot of people—most people—don't know this, but…"

He paused, waiting.

I had no choice but to take the bait. "What, Chancellor?"

His eyes gleamed. "Aliens."

I blinked. "…Aliens?"

He nodded, completely serious. "Extraterrestrials. They've been here before. Millennia ago. They built the pyramids, you know. A lot of people don't know that. And they've been watching us ever since. Waiting."

I stared at him, willing my expression to remain

professional. What in the actual hell was I supposed to do with this? He leaned back, sighing deeply. The chair groaned beneath his weight.

"Of course, the liberals will tell you that's ridiculous. You know who else will? The Catholics."

My fingers twitched against my tablet. "The… Catholics?"

He nodded gravely. "Oh yes. The Vatican has known about the alien presence for centuries. Why do you think they have their own observatory? You don't know this, but the Pope has been in contact with them since the 1600s. It's all part of their plan."

I swallowed. This was going to be a long interview.

"Of course, that's only one front," Callus continued, rubbing a thumb along his pudgy chin, wiping away some of the badly applied concealer. "There's another. One far more dangerous."

I didn't even need to ask this time.

"The Gay Agenda," he declared.

My stomach sank.

"You'll be as surprised to learn as I was," he said, "that the goal of the trans movement is not equality. Oh, no. No, no, no. It's control. If you can make people believe a man is a woman, that a woman is a man, that up is down, that day is night, then what can't you make them believe?"

He tapped his sausage-like fingers against the desk, emphasizing his point.

"If you can erase the truth of biological reality, then you can erase anything. History. Government. Me."

His voice tightened, his expression suddenly haunted, as if the greatest threat to his rule was pronouns. I'm going to have to delete ninety percent of this interview, I thought.

Three hours later, I sat alone in my apartment, staring at the footage. It was a disaster. The video jumped from topic to topic, an unhinged stream-of-consciousness rant about conspiracies so wild they would have been funny, if they weren't coming from the most powerful man in the city. I ran my hands down my face. There had to be something usable. I scrubbed through the footage, deleting huge sections, cutting together what little I could. The final result was awkwardly stitched together, a Frankenstein's monster of an interview where Callus appeared to be answering questions I asked. The reality was I dubbed in my questions to make some semblance of order out of his ramblings. It was the only thing I could.

The next morning, I submitted my piece.

CHANCELLOR CALLUS:
VISIONARY FOR A NEW AGE

It was one of the most widely distributed interviews in history.

I have never been more ashamed of my own work.

Chapter 11

THE GHOST NETWORK

Adam led me to the center of his operations. I had imagined something crude—a bunker crammed with desperate dissidents, huddled over dimly lit tables, whispering rebellion in hushed, frantic voices. I had pictured a war room of sorts, walls plastered with cryptic messages and half-baked conspiracy theories, a place held together by paranoia and desperation. But this? This was something else entirely.

The air was thick with the quiet pulse of machinery, the steady thrum of overworked servers and cooling fans struggling to keep pace. The glow of multiple monitors bathed the room in an eerie blue haze, casting long, jagged shadows against walls lined with salvaged tech. Rows of mismatched terminals, their casings cracked and mismatched, as lines of code scrolled across the screens—live data feeds, intercepted transmissions, backdoor scripts running in real-time. The setup was a patchwork of stolen ingenuity. Black-market servers wired together with repurposed military hardware. Pirated software bending the rules of cyberspace in ways I could barely comprehend. Someone had taken the scraps of a broken world and built something dangerous, something powerful, out of them.

And his team—hunched over workstations, eyes reflecting lines of data as fingers moved in rapid precision across keyboards. They weren't nervous. They weren't frantic. They were focused. Calculated. I realized then—this wasn't chaos. This was control.

This was the Ghost Network. I had somehow taken it to mean a network of individuals. I see now it was quite literally a network. A fully operational, underground system. Adam had built an empire out of scraps. And somehow, it was still running.

I turned to him in astonishment. "You did all this?"

He smiled. "What, expecting a cave with candles and a conspiracy board?"

I scoffed. "Maybe a few walls covered in red string. Some 'Down with The Leader' posters."

Adam chuckled. "We're not anarchists, Iris. We're engineers. If you want to tear something down, first you have to understand how it works so it can be rebuilt."

I stepping further inside. The space was big but not vast—just enough for a handful of people to work undisturbed. Two other Ghosts sat at workstations, their faces illuminated by the glow of the monitors. Neither one looked up. They were focused. Efficient. Invisible to the world above. Just like me. I turned back to Adam.

"So, tell me something."

He arched an eyebrow. "Go on."

"If you and I are ghosts now—erased from the

system, our SES gone, our existence wiped—then why does it matter? Why are worried about being found?"

Adam's expression didn't change, but something in his posture shifted.

I pressed on. "Hollis, Rayne, The Board—they shouldn't be able to find us. If the system doesn't see us, we've already won. Haven't we?"

For a moment, Adam said nothing. Then, with slow precision, he leaned against the nearest workstation, arms folded.

"Have you ever deleted a file, Iris?"

I frowned. "Obviously."

"And what happens after you delete it?"

I opened my mouth, then stopped.

He waited.

"It sits in the trash bin. Until you empty it."

Adam nodded. "And even then, the data's not actually gone, is it?"

I waited for him to answer his own question.

"You know what really happens when you delete something?" Adam continued. "You're telling the system it doesn't exist anymore. But the data? It's still there. Hidden in the storage background, waiting to be overwritten only if the space is needed."

Realization settled over me like ice.

Adam continued, his voice quieter now.

"The system will eventually notice the discrepancy in our final processing. It will need to correct the logic error. It is infallible, you know."

I inhaled sharply. "You're saying the Algorithm is trying to find us as well?"

He nodded. "Right now, it's running the numbers. Trying to process why some assets flagged for offloading were already coded final asset process before the other commands could be run."

I shivered at the thought of an artificial intelligence hunting us. "And if it figures it out?"

Adam met my gaze. "Not if...when. It will reinstate us, then process us correctly. For real this time."

A heavy silence settled between us. For a brief moment, I had allowed myself to believe we had already won. That by slipping through the cracks, we had escaped. But of course a perfect system wasn't going to fall for it it. It would correct itself. Between that, and Evelyn Rayne and Hollis...

"Damn" I sighed.

The words hidden in the background, waiting to be overwritten echoed in my head.

I turned to Adam. "Couldn't we just—overwrite the files ourselves?"

He didn't flinch. He had been expecting the question. "That's exactly what we're trying to do."

He gestured toward the Ghosts hunched over their monitors, faces bathed in the soft glow of cascading code.

"We are in a race" Adam continued, "they're combing through layers of buried system data, hunting down our existence. If we can get to it first—wipe every record, every flagged process, every redundancy—we can truly erase ourselves."

I exhaled, feeling a flicker of hope. "Then we have a chance."

Adam's smirk was gone now. "-IF- we find it first. And that's a bigger if than you might imagine. We have to find all versions. There may be millions of data points in the built-in redundancies. I know, I wrote many of the protocols myself. You have to put in a lot of fail-safes to create the perfect 'infallible' Algorithm."

I frowned. "And it doesn't?"

"The system only needs to find one version." His expression darkened. "Then the Algorithm can complete its logical correction. It locates the discrepancy, restores our data, reinstates our files, and finishes the job. Final Asset Processing."

It wasn't a simple delete command. We were up against an intelligence designed to be infallible. A machine built to anticipate, adapt, and correct. A system that had already decided we didn't belong. I turned back to Adam.

I straightened. "And if you don't find them soon. Do you have a Plan B?"

Adam held my gaze.

"You're it."

It was obvious I didn't understand.

"We need to give it a bigger problem to solve. If we can expose your files, get your stories planted, get the system working on defending Callus and resolving threats your files will pose, it will put its energy there, and put finding us on low priority."

"You don't think it can do both?" I asked.

His face did not reflect much confidence. "Yeah— well, that's the plan, anyway."

Chapter 12

LAW AND ORDER IN THE UNDERCITY

The next morning Adam showed me another facet of life in the Undercity. He led me to a place in the market area where he spent time among the offloaded, trying to give them a little bit of decency and self-respect while they were trapped down here. The Undercity market was alive in its own way, not bustling like the manufactured streets of New Columbia, but pulsing—a slow, rhythmic heartbeat of desperation and necessity. Stalls lined the narrow walkways, their makeshift tables weighed down with scavenged goods: rusted tools, repurposed electronics, threadbare clothing carefully patched for another round of wear. The air smelled of sweat and burning plastic, a sharp contrast to the sterile, perfumed air of the city above. Fires burned in scattered barrels, their glow casting flickering shadows against the tunnel walls, dancing over the faces of the forgotten. Adam and I sat at a small wooden table, little more than a crate and a few salvaged chairs. The table was covered in an assortment of scraps of wire, gears and miscellaneous hardware someone might make use of. Adam wasn't worried about turning it into money, it was more of a cover for his philanthropic efforts.

Across from us, an elderly woman carefully poured something that resembled tea into two mismatched cups. The scent was earthy, bitter. Adam thanked her with a nod, sliding a few barter tokens across the table in exchange. I cupped my hands around the warmth of my drink, watching as a young boy, barely ten, worked beside the woman, arranging small bundles of herbs for sale. He was silent, efficient, moving with the practiced motions of someone who had learned to survive by blending into the background.

"You come here to help these people?" I asked, voice low.

Adam rubbed a thumb along the rim of his cup. "We do what we can."

I waited, sensing there was more.

He glanced around, his eyes scanning the market—not just watching, but seeing. His gaze lingered on a group of offloaded huddled near a vendor selling bowls of rice and protein paste. Their faces were hollow, their movements slow. A lifetime of exhaustion.

"Most of them don't belong here," Adam said finally. "Not really."

"I thought the Algorithm only removes those who deserve it." My words were edged with sarcasm.

Adam made a face that looked like he might be amused, but there was no humor in it. "And I thought you reporter types knew the truth behind the lies."

He shifted in his chair, lowering his voice as he leaned toward me. "Can you imagine believing that this many people—all of them—are guilty of some crime? That an entire city's worth of men, women, and children are so evil and twisted that the protectors of society were able to tell from their SES that they are worthless—less than human?"

I said nothing.

"The system needs workers," he continued. "Cheap, replaceable, invisible workers. Offloading isn't about crime. It's about supply and demand."

I looked back at the boy sorting herbs.

"Child labor," I murmured.

Adam nodded grimly. "Age doesn't matter. The Board needs factories, assembly lines, mines, waste processors. They need people desperate enough to work for nothing. People who won't complain, won't strike, won't fight back—because they believe they deserve to be here."

A hollow ache spread through my thoughts, the sharp sting of realizing the truth I had helped spread was nothing more than propaganda to support a lie. I scowled.

Adam must have seen the shift in my expression because his voice softened. "Those of us that can—we try to remind them that they're more than numbers. That they still have value."

He gestured subtly toward the vendor beside us, where a woman carefully sanded down salvaged wooden doors and dividers, polishing them into something resembling craftsmanship. A pointless endeavor in a place where privacy was a luxury no one could afford. But she worked anyway. And the way she straightened when she caught someone admiring her work—just for a second—told me he was right. A small thing. A pointless thing. And yet— It meant something. To her. I opened my mouth to say something, but Adam's entire posture changed. His shoulders stiffened. His jaw tightened.

"Iris, do me a favor, Make yourself scarce for a minute," he muttered, waving a hand to dismiss me.

I followed his gaze. A man was moving through the stalls. He moved like a jackal picking through the bones of a carcass, slow and methodical. Three men flanking him. I slipped off the crate, moving quietly behind the stall beside ours. The woman sanding the wooden doors didn't acknowledge me, but saw me. I pressed myself into the shadows, watching.

Adam didn't move as Rezik approached. Rezik swaggered through the rows of scavenged goods, his coat still too clean, his boots barely worn, his posture screaming someone who hadn't learned yet. Newly offloaded. Fresh from New Columbia's false promises and corporate arrogance. And already looking for a way to crawl back to power. Adam didn't acknowledge him right away. Didn't need to. He'd seen the Reziks before, knew what Rezik was before Rezik even opened his mouth.

I would later learn that Rezik Vance had been in the Undercity less than a week. Freshly offloaded, dumped into the abyss like so many others before him. A former corporate enforcer, stripped of his SES, dumped into the Undercity without warning, without resources, without power. A man who didn't know his place yet. And just as we in the news business had always promoted, he assumed this place was lawless. That the strong did what they wanted. That the weak had no choice but to kneel.

Seeing Adam, an old man, sitting helpless at a vendor's booth, he thought he had spotted one of the weak ones. Adam looked pretty defenseless, hunched in a chair, dressed in the rags that had once been fine clothes. To Rezik, Adam appeared to be some downtrodden scavenger, barely scraping by, selling junk that wasn't worth stealing.

And yet, Rezik noticed, he was wearing a watch. A simple thing, strapped to his wrist. Not digital. Not smart-tech. Just a sturdy analog timepiece, the kind built in the days before the Algorithm ruled lives. A relic. A treasure. And to Rezik's way of thinking, a man like Adam had no business having a treasure in his kingdom.

Rezik moved in for the kill.

Rezik had nothing left from his life above. If he could get his hands on something worth trading ... That watch could get him a knife. Or a ration card. Or a fix of something to take the edge off. So he made a calculated decision.

Like so many before him, he made the wrong one.

Rezik stepped up to the stall, hands in his coat pockets, chin lifted just slightly. The stance of a man trying to look bigger than he was. Adam didn't look up.

Adam turned a small metal gear in his fingers, inspecting the teeth with absent patience, all the while watching, measuring this intruder..

Rezik let his gaze skim over the scattered electronics, the tiny assortment of parts. Nothing valuable. Nothing worth stealing. Except for the watch, and the stall-keeper still hadn't acknowledged him. Rezik smiled to himself. Easy mark. He leaned against the table, knocking a few circuit boards to the floor with his elbow.

"You sell anything besides garbage?" he asked, tone mocking.

Adam's gray eyes were calm, unreadable. Not annoyed. Not nervous. Just…observational. Rezik felt something small and unpleasant stir in his gut. But he shoved it down.

"How about that?" he asked, reaching for the watch. "How much?"

Adam pulled his arm back from Rezik's reach.

"Not for sale."

Rezik snorted.

"Great, I'll take it."

Adam tilted his head slightly. "I said its not for sale."

Rezik's grin twitched.

"I didn't say I was going to buy it."

Adam didn't answer. Just held his gaze. Rezik's instincts told him he was dealing with someone more than a stall owner, he realized he wasn't reading the old man right. Yet his greed pushed him on. He was too hungry, too desperate, too angry to stop himself. He grunted, straightening, calling the man's bluff.

"Tell you what. I'll do you a favor," Rezik snarled.

Adam raised an eyebrow. "Is that so?"

"Yeah," Rezik said, grinning. "Hand over the watch and I won't break your neck."

Adam didn't shift his gaze. In the Undercity, a working watch could be bartered for a week's worth of food. Rezik's men stood back uncomfortably, shifting from one foot to the other, posturing like vultures waiting for the kill. Adam's heavy sigh increased their discomfort. The old man obviously felt this was a waste of his time.

"I think you might have the wrong impression of where you are," Adam said mildly.

Rezik chuckled. "Do I?"

"You don't understand the first thing about what happens in the Undercity."

"I understand plenty."

Rezik turned slightly, scanning the cluster of huddled figures nearby—weak, sick, too exhausted to move.

"The strong take what they need," Rezik said, stepping toward one of them. "And the weak—" Rezik drew a rusty blade from his coat and laid it against the cheek of the frightened woman sitting nearby. The point drew a small drop of blood from the paper-thin skin of her cheekbone. He reached down and picked up her cup of tea, adding "The weak give it to the strong."

Adam calmly made a slight motion with his fingers. The motion was subtle. Not excited. Not angry. Just the slow motion of two fingers raised, then lowered. Suddenly Rezik wasn't standing anymore. The thug was on his knees, choking, eyes wide with terror. A blade was at his throat. Not just a blade. A shining stainless steel army blade, serrated teeth hovering against the pulse of his neck. The hand holding it belonged to a man no one had noticed before. Lean, quiet, with the unreadable patience of a predator. The market went silent.

Rezik's eyes bounced, taking in the situation. Surrounding him and his men, a dozen knives were suddenly present.

Adam sighed, rubbing the bridge of his nose. "You really should've done your own homework before handing out assignments." he said.

Rezik's bravado shattered - helpless and one wrong breath from losing his life.

"I—" he stammered. Adam raised his finger slightly. The blade pressed closer. Rezik made a choking sound, barely holding still. His face lost its color. His men stood motionless, too afraid to act. Adam let the moment stretch. Long enough for Rezik to understand. Then with another flip of his wrist, he waved off the attack. The blade lowered. Rezik stumbling back gasping for air.

Adam leaned forward, elbows on his knees, expression unreadable. He reached forward and removed the rusted blade from Reziks trembling hand. The old woman scrambled to get away. Adam held the rusted blade up, turning it from side to side in front of Rezik's face.

"Do go on ...You were saying something about understanding plenty?"

Rezik didn't speak. Couldn't. His confidence had

just bled out onto the dirt.

Adam took his time, studying him.

"You don't take from me," he said with the finality of a father scolding a child. "You don't take from them." He nodded toward the huddled figures Rezik had tried to intimidate. "And you never – ever – mistake my kindness for weakness."

Silence. Then, carefully, Rezik stood. His jaw clenched. His hands rubbed his neck where the blade had been pressed. And then—he nodded. Not much. Barely a fraction. But enough. Adam nodded back.

"Good," Adam said. "Now let's talk about what you can do to make yourself useful around here."

Rezik was many things. Proud. Opportunistic. Brutal. But he wasn't stupid. He had come into the Undercity thinking it was chaos. Thinking power belonged to the loudest voice, the strongest hands. But real power was quiet. Organized. It moves in shadows and whispers in darkness. And it had just showed itself to him.

Rezik straightened, clearing his throat, forcing himself to speak.

"What do you want from me?"

Adam smiled, slow and patient.

"You want to run things down here?" he asked. "Fine. I'm not going to stand in your way. But not if you're going to act like some thug shaking down the helpless. You want real power? Then protect the ones who can't protect themselves. Make yourself valuable. But be careful of who you press. Because if you don't—"

His smile faded.

"You won't be found."

Rezik exhaled through his nose and stepped back. His men were already looking at him differently. Like a man who had been given a single choice. He swallowed hard, then—slowly—he nodded.

"Alright," he said. "Alright."

Adam leaned back in his chair, satisfied. "Now get the hell out of my sight."

Rezik left, his men trailing behind him, shaken but alive. The market din returned. Adam shook his head, rubbing his temples and looked over to me. He lifted his cup of tea and held it out to me, motioning me to come back and join him. I stepped back out from my hiding place and sat down next to Adam, letting out a long extended breath.

"Well!" I huffed. "I didn't see that coming!"

He remained seated at the table, watching the space Rezik had just vacated. His fingers tapped idly against the surface, his expression unreadable.

I shifted in my seat. "I have questions."

Adam squinted, and smiled. his face still calm, even after the show he had put on. "I'm sure you do."

"Those men— the ones who came out of nowhere to your defense." I gestured vaguely toward the market. "Who the hell where they? Are they your Ghosts?"

Adam shook his head. "No."

I frowned. "Unless I'm missing something, you just had a small army at your back"

Adam exhaled, stretching his fingers against the tabletop. "They're offloaded. Just like everyone else down here."

That wasn't the answer I wanted. "Maybe" I said slowly, "but they seemed a bit organized wouldn't you agree? Why did they stand up for you?"

He turned his gaze to the market, scanning the makeshift stalls, the vendors hawking their salvaged tech and black-market scraps.

"Because they still remember," he said simply.

I blinked. "Remember what?"

His gaze flicked back to me. "What it was like to have structure. To have control over their own lives. The Algorithm may have convinced them they belong here, but it doesn't erase their needs. They may not want to escape—but they do want a certain amount of security."

"And they think that you can provide that?"

Adam nodded. "The Board built the Undercity to be a wasteland. A punishment. When the offloaded arrive, they expect chaos—dog-eat-dog, survival of the fittest. The strong preying on the weak, keeping them too desperate, too broken to ever resist. It's the first thing the neurotransmitter feed them, hopelessness. The idea that there is nothing here for them. The designers wanted the offloaded to be willing, desperate. Compliant workers."

He set his tea cup on the table and smoothed the paper it sat on absentmindedly. "But that's not how people work."

I frowned. "Go on."

Adam's eyes sharpened. "No matter how much they believe they deserve this, they - we all - still cling to the only thing that keeps us all alive—each other.

We're not forcing anything on anyone. But when we saw that we could start carving out some semblance of stability, when we made it possible for people to survive without turning on each other, it resonated with their natural instincts. Most people want to be part of something, to belong."

I let out a slow breath.

Adam hadn't just managed to survive in the Undercity. He'd reorganized it.

"Then why the hell did you turn Rezik loose? You basically told him to take over."

"I did."

"Why?"

Adam leaned forward, crossing his forearms on the table. "Because he needs to believe he has power."

I scoffed. "You just told me you spent years stopping people like him. Now you're handing him control of this market? He's a petty thief and a would be shake-down artist."

Adam shook his head. "I gave him a role. And offered no control."

I waited, studying his face carefully, while he continued.

"People like Rezik come down here thinking they're about to become warlords. They think the Undercity is lawless, a free-for-all where the strongest rule. And in the early days, that was true. But not anymore. We spent years forcing structure into a world designed to be unstructured. Not just to make life bearable—but because we need it."

"Because." He hesitated, his voice dropped

slightly. "We can't function in chaos."

I stiffened. "We" The Ghost Network. Their desire to take down the Oligarchs, to break the Algorithm and SES ratings.

"Are you trying to make the Undercity some kind of model for a new society?"

Adam didn't confirm or deny it. "We're fighting a system built on control, on efficiency, on absolute obedience. If we don't have a working system of our own, we don't stand a chance. We need order just as much as they do. Maybe even more."

I stared at him, my mind turning over his words.

I had assumed the Ghosts were just surviving down here, hiding, waiting for an opportunity to overthrow the system. But now I began to suspect that that wasn't the full plan.

Adam exhaled, continuing where he left off about why he released Rezik and his thugs.

"Rezik is a tool. He wants power, so I let him think he has some. He'll take his role seriously now. Keep the stalls in check, keep the violence contained, enforce his own rules. And in the process, we maintain order without lifting a finger."

I shook my head. "He could still cause damage."

Adam's mouth curled into something almost amused. "True. enough, he can," he shrugged. "But then he'll have to deal with my army again. Checks and balances."

I turned my gaze back to the market, watching the vendors haggle, the offloaded going about their lives, not realizing that they were living in a world Adam had quietly built around them. Rezik had thought he could assume control through fear and strength. But the real power was sitting across from me. Quiet, unassuming, Adam Solace was a much bigger player in the game than I had thought.

I was still processing everything Adam had told me when I noticed someone weaving through the crowd. At first, I thought the person was just another vendor, peddling whatever scraps they had scavenged. As the person neared, their eyes darted left, then right, scanning the space for eavesdroppers. Their gaze landed on Adam.

"You're going to want to see this," they murmured, voice low but urgent. "Clarence found something."

Adam's expression sharpened. He nodded.

"Lee," he greeted them, noffing towards me. "This is—"

"We've met," I interrupted, smiling slightly.

Adam's gaze flicked between us, intrigued.

"Oh? When was this?"

"Earlier, this morning," I said, glancing at Lee. "In the bathhouse."

Lee and I shared a knowing look as we both recalled the encounter.

Steam curled in soft ribbons through the dimly lit space, the scent of damp stone mixing with something faintly herbal—some kind of scavenged soap, maybe. The bathhouse was small and bare-bones, just a few stalls partitioned by old scrap metal and patched fabric curtains, but it was one of the few places in the Undercity that gave the illusion of normalcy. I had just finished rinsing off, still toweling my hair dry, when I stepped into the changing area and saw someone already there, pulling on a coat. I froze instinctively, caught off guard by the unexpected company. The person had turned at the movement, their expression easy. They offered a small, lopsided smile, holding up their hands in a gesture of harmlessness.

"Sorry. Didn't realize someone else was here."

The tone was casual, but I still hesitated, tightening my grip on my towel. They remained casual, unbothered by my awkwardness. After making some adjustments to the waist band of their coat, they... I couldn't tell if it was a man or woman, leaned against the changing room wall, giving me space but making no move to leave. I took the moment to assess them—short, solid build, sharp features softened by an easy confidence. Their buzzed hair was still damp, droplets clinging to their temple. They weren't in any hurry.

"I'm Iris" I offered.

"I'm Lee. You new?" Lee asked.

"Something like that," I replied cautiously.

Lee huffed a quiet laugh. "Figured. You look like you still think this place isn't real."

That caught me off guard. I nodded. "Yeah, a little."

A shrug. "Most offloaded spend their first few weeks acting like this is some bad dream they'll wake up from. You're still in that stage. But give it time."

I studied them a little closer, trying to place them

in the strange hierarchy of the Undercity.

"And you accept this place as reality then?"

Another small smirk. "Its better than my old reality."

I tilted my head. "You're… okay with being down here?"

Lee hesitated for a fraction of a second, then nodded. "I mean, look around. Everyone here's got something, right? A failure, a mistake, a reason they got dropped. Nobody's perfect, but up there, you're expected to be. Down here? You just are. It's the first place I've been where I don't feel out of place."

That was new. Every other offloaded I had met clung desperately to the idea that they didn't belong here. That they were different. That there had been a mistake. But this person—

I hesitated, choosing my words carefully. "What do you mean by 'out of place'?"

Lee studied me for a moment before answering. "I mean that in New Columbia, the system wants everything in neat little boxes. Unfortunately I didn't fit into any of them."

There was something pointed in the way it was phrased.

Understanding clicked into place.

"What are your pronouns?" I asked.

Lee grinned slightly. "They/Them."

I nodded, thinking about the way it had been presented. Like saying the sky is blue or water is wet. Lee wasn't asking for permission or demanding acknowledgment. Just stating what was.

"I take it is easier down here to be non-binary?" I asked.

Lee shrugged. "It is and it isn't. But down here, most everyone's too busy surviving to worry about what I call myself."

"As opposed to up there?"

Lee scoffed. "Up there, people like me are a problem. The Algorithm doesn't like what it can't categorize. And if the system doesn't know what to do with you, it finds a way to get rid of you."

I had nothing to say to that. I'd seen it happen—people who didn't fit, whose existence was an inconvenience to the structure of New Columbia. The system didn't offload them outright. It just downgraded their score with each infraction, until... offload.

Lee gave me a two-fingered salute and grabbed their satchel. "See you around, city girl."

I grinned at Lee as I snapped back to the present. "I was wondering where I'd see you again."

Lee smirked. "Yeah? Well I certainly didn't peg you as someone who'd be hanging out sipping tea with the big boss." They motioned to Adam.

Adam raised an eyebrow. "You two seem to have hit it off."

Lee shrugged. "She didn't try to stab me, so yeah, we're good."

I rolled my eyes

"So, Clarence found something?" Adam brought

us back to the moment.

Lee's expression shifted, the easy humor draining away.

"Yes, and he wants you to come right away."

The walk to the Ghost Network's headquarters wound through a labyrinth of back alleys, abandoned tunnels, and repurposed corridors deep within the Undercity. It wasn't a single place, I realized, but a network of hidden rooms and corridors stitched together like an underground nervous system—carefully concealed, constantly shifting, impossible to track.

As we walked, Adam gestured toward Lee.

"They don't look it, but they're one of my best code writers," he said.

Lee scoffed. "Gee, thanks. Really selling me there, boss."

Adam smirked. "Just saying. Don't let the age or good looks fool you."

I glanced at Lee, who looked barely older than twenty.

"How did you get involved in all this?"

Lee shrugged. "Adam needed someone who could think outside the Algorithm's rules. Turns out, that's kind of my specialty."

I believed it.

We reached the entrance—an unmarked door between two derelict stalls, disguised as another dead end in the labyrinth of the Undercity. Adam punched in a code on a rusted keypad. The lock clicked, and we slipped inside. Dim lights cast long shadows over exposed wiring and patched-up server racks. The air was thick with the shush of cooling fans and the acrid scent of solder. Clarence was waiting inside. He was young—messy brown hair, sharp eyes that burned with the kind of intensity only people with something to prove ever had. He saw us, then grinned like he'd been sitting on the best secret in the world.

"I found a way into the news reporting funnel," he beamed. "Iris, I understand you have some data you'd like to release discreetly?"

Chapter 13

CAPT. RAYNE'S ASSIGNMENT

Outside the bookstore, I was still lost in thought wondering how Iris had eluded me once again. The bookstore had been a dead-end, and now it would be some time before the LIDAR came back. I turned for home, thinking Milo's attention might be the distraction I needed, when my watch buzzed.

REPORT TO ISB

The Internal Security Bureau or ISB as it was called, stood at the very heart of New Columbia—both in geography and in power. It loomed in the center of the Executive District, its structure a monolith of black glass and reinforced steel, rising high above the city's lower tiers. Unlike the Corporate Board's headquarters, which radiated opulence, the ISB tower was pure function—a fortress of control. It had no windows. No identifying marks. No banners of loyalty, no slogans of unity. It didn't need them. Everyone already knew what it was.

The ISB was the hand of the Algorithm, the enforcers of its will—the final authority on who belonged in society, and who did not. It was the one institution feared more than the enforcers themselves. And as I walked through its cold, metallic corridors, I felt that fear settling in my bones.

Before New Columbia, before the Algorithm, before Callus, there had been other agencies. The CIA. FBI. NSA. Relics of a government that once swore to protect its people. But after the fall of democracy, those institutions collapsed under the weight of their own inefficiencies. When the economic failures reached a breaking point—when crime, corruption, and so-called "civil liberties" had driven society into chaos—a new solution was required. And Callus provided it.

When he rose to power, he dismantled the broken intelligence agencies and replaced them with something pure, singular, absolute—the Internal Security Bureau. No jurisdictional disputes. No bureaucratic delays. Just one entity with one function—to enforce the Algorithm's will.

It began as an intelligence division, but over time, its reach expanded. Surveillance. Every citizen was watched, tracked, analyzed. Offloading. Those deemed unworthy were erased, removed without hesitation. Recalibration. Those who could be corrected were sent to be reshaped.

The ISB controlled who lived and who disappeared. And the one who ruled over it? Director Marius Locke. Locke was not Callus. He wasn't a public figure, not a man who gave speeches or inspired loyalty. He was unseen, unspoken, but ever-present. A name spoken in hushed tones, feared in silence. He had been handpicked by Callus himself, chosen for his unwavering devotion to order.

While Callus was the voice of New Columbia, Locke was the executioner. It was said that not even Callus questioned Locke's methods. Because to Locke, loyalty was not measured in words, but in absolute obedience. And it was Locke who decided who was a liability, a threat to the system. People feared Callus. They obeyed the Algorithm. But they prayed never to hear their name spoken by the ISB.

"Why is Delacroix still out there, Captain Rayne?"

Director Marius Locke's voice was as smooth as polished steel. Controlled. Unshaken. Dangerous. I had been expecting this conversation. I stood before his stark glass desk, hands clasped behind my back in parade-rest, stance crisp, disciplined. The LIDAR scan results glowed in the air between us, casting shifting lines of red and green across Locke's face. The man didn't blink.

"She accessed an unauthorized exit point," I said, voice neutral. "A hidden passage from the bookstore into the Undercity."

Locke's fingers steepled. "And yet, the Watchers have nothing on her."

I hesitated briefly weighing the consequences of admitting it. "That's correct, sir."

Locke tilted his head slightly. "Explain."

I flicked my wrist, pulling up Iris Delacroix's last known movements. The final Watcher log. The moment her record ceased to exist and pointed to the last entry.

FINAL ASSET PROCESS COMPLETE

Silence. A slow, deliberate tap of Locke's finger against the desk.

"That," he paused, "shouldn't be possible, Captain."

"No, sir," I agreed. "It should not."

The Algorithm never made mistakes. And yet, somehow, a woman who was alive, who had just been seen entering an unauthorized access point, had suddenly been marked as processed. As if she had never existed. As if something—or someone—had erased her. Locke was silent for a long moment, fingers pressed together, his gaze dissecting the LIDAR scans between us. I waited, still as stone. Then, finally—he exhaled slowly, almost pleased.

"Don't look so defeated, Captain," he said, tapping the floating holo-display, "this is the first real proof we've had."

I forced myself not to react, but I felt a wave of relief wash over me. Locke hadn't called me in to grill me on Delacroix. He has something else in mind. I was still juggling the thought of how Delacroix had been erased when Locke refocused my attention on him.

"This is unauthorized bio-metric data removal, Captain," Locke continued. "Someone is tampering with The Algorithm's records. This is subversion."

A surge of adrenaline pulsed through me. He shifted the display, and a list of names flickered into view. My stomach clenched.

Scheduled for Offloading. Disappeared. No Finalization Data.

Delacroix wasn't the only one. Dozens. Dozens of names, all flagged for removal—all missing.

"This is not an isolated incident," Locke said smoothly, but there was an edge of something darker underneath. "We have been tracking a pattern. People flagged for offloading who… simply vanish. Their records do not transition. They do not show up in the Undercity's census logs."

His gaze lifted to mine.

"They have escaped justice."

I kept my expression unreadable, but my pulse quickened. A pattern. This wasn't a glitch—it was an operation.

"Until now," Locke continued, "these anomalies were dismissed as acceptable deviation. The Algorithm processes millions of citizens daily. A few missing records? Statistical noise."

"But this isn't noise," I said quietly.

"No," Locke confirmed. "Not when it's deliberate."

He adjusted the display, and the data stream shifted again. I frowned. The next set of figures wasn't people. It was code. A series of undecipherable symbols and numbers flashed in a long chain of sequence. Presumably meaningful to someone or something, but not intelligible to the common person, I watched for a moment. confusion growing on my face.

"Please explain," I said.

"This," Locke said, gesturing to the fragmented sequences, "is data leakage."

I stiffened. He let the words hang, watching me.

"We've been tracking irregular data flows originating from the Undercity," he continued. "At first, they were dismissed—fragmented transmissions, discarded system noise. But these anomalies aren't random. They're coordinated."

A cold ripple spread through me.

"Meaning?"

"Meaning," Locke said, "someone is pushing encrypted bursts of information through the system. And we cannot locate the source."

That sent a deep, cutting thrill down my spine. The Undercity wasn't supposed to have infrastructure capable of digital subversion. The offloaded weren't supposed to have anything. But if someone had built a network down there—an organized, structured resistance—My mind raced.

"If this is encryption," I said slowly, "we should have been able to intercept something by now."

Locke groaned slightly.

"Oh, we have."

Another flick of his fingers, and a distorted audio recording played through the room. The words were garbled, broken by static and digital scrambling. I strained to pick out a pattern.

"It repeats," Locke said. "At random intervals, different locations, always just above the interference threshold of the surveillance grid. We believe it's some kind of command signal. Possibly coordinating movement. Possibly something else."

My pulse pounded. This was not just a breach.

This was warfare. And up until now, we hadn't even realized it was happening. Locke leaned back, his gaze settling on me.

"This is the moment, Rayne." His voice shifted, growing colder. Sharper. Purposeful.

"This is where we turn the tide."

He paused, then let his voice harden.

"New Columbia is a beacon." He spoke slowly, deliberately. Pressing. "A civilization built on order, efficiency, strength. And we will not allow parasites to fester in its shadow."

Something flared in my chest.

Yes.

"You understand now, don't you?" Locke continued. "This is not just about a missing journalist. This is about the survival of New Columbia itself."

I met his gaze.

"Sir, what are my orders?"

A stern look spread across his face.

"You will be inserted into the Undercity," he said. "Find these ghosts. Find Delacroix. Find the network."

A hunt. Not just for one woman. For all of them. I straightened.

"Understood, sir."

Locke nodded. Then, after a pause, he added—

"And Captain?"

I met his gaze.

"Do not underestimate them." His voice was calm, smooth, but there was something sharp underneath. "They have already eluded us this long. Which means they are not weak."

I gave a crisp nod. That was fine. Neither was I.

———————————————————————————

I arrived at the ISB's covert operations division just after nightfall. No time to waste. The debrief room was colder than the rest of the building, the air controlled to near-sterile precision. A single steel table, six chairs, and five men and women already seated. I recognized them. The best infiltration specialists the ISB had to offer. None of them spoke when I entered, but their eyes sized me up instantly. At the head of the table, Commander Dain Juric leaned back in his chair, his fingers drumming against the surface. He had the hollowed-out look of a man who had spent too long staring at screens, too long listening to the secrets of the world. His SES was well above 6.0, meaning he was more trusted than most.

He nodded as I took my seat.

"We've finalized your insertion plan, Captain."

I looked at him, a feeling of anticipation and excitement welling within me. "Let's hear it."

Juric tapped the console, and a dossier flickered to life on the table's embedded display. A woman's face appeared—thin, drawn, eyes empty with defeat.

"You will go in as one Marla Sedgewick. Office drone, Level 2 procurement clerk. SES: 2.3 before she was flagged for inefficiency. Dropped to 1.9 after termination."

I studied the profile carefully. She was real. Or, at least, she had been.

"Where is the real Sedgewick?" I asked.

Juric barely looked up. "Final Processing." His voice was flat, clinical. "Her offloading was expedited this morning. She is being held until your insertion. Once the transition is complete, she will be... finalized."

Finalized. I knew what that meant. She wouldn't just be offloaded. She wouldn't be left to scrape by in the gutters of the Undercity, clawing for scraps among the forgotten. She would be terminated. No body. No burial. No record that she had ever lived. Just another bureaucratic adjustment. A seamless replacement.

I nodded once, sharp and decisive. No hesitation. No second thoughts.

"Necessary losses," I reminded myself.

Marla was a single defective unit, already slated for deletion. And in her place, I would walk freely into the Undercity, slip beneath its skin, and excise the infection festering there. One life for the security of millions. One soul sacrificed so that the disease of dissent could be eradicated. That was the equation. That was the logic. It was justified. Wasn't it? I inhaled slowly, steadying my pulse. This was the cost of order. The price of strength. And yet...

For the briefest second, I glanced at her picture. I saw her eyes. I wondered who she loved, who would mourn her. A flicker of something unfamiliar twisted in my chest. Something restless. Something I didn't like. I ignored it. I had a mission. I had a war to win. Sedgewick was already gone. And now, I would become her.

"The drones will offload you tomorrow at 05:30,"

Juric continued. "You will arrive as a standard civilian removal. No special markers, no modified transport routes. We need this to look real."

"Understood," I said.

"Your primary objective is reconnaissance," Juric said. "You are not to engage. You are not to make contact unless absolutely necessary."

That was expected.

"If there is an organized resistance, they have managed to evade our surveillance for years," he continued. "Which means they are cautious, disciplined, and deeply embedded. You will have one shot at integrating without drawing suspicion. If they suspect you're an outsider, they will disappear."

"What are my first steps?" I asked.

"Follow standard offloading protocols. Find shelter. Observe. You will likely be approached by one of the Underworld's self-proclaimed 'street lords.' They control resources. Protection. You will play the part of someone desperate for survival."

I frowned. "And my extraction?"

Juric glanced at the woman to his right—Chief Tech Officer Sera Lin. She was the only person in the room whose SES came close to Locke's.

"We will provide you with a concealed beacon," she said. "A passive-frequency chip embedded in your molar. No active signals, nothing the locals can detect."

I clenched my jaw. "And navigation?"

Lin's lips curled slightly.

"The Algorithm's Geo-positioning grid still

reaches the Undercity, but no standard citizen has access to it. You, however, will have a limited decryption module. It will overlay navigation data onto your retinal HUD."

I raised an eyebrow. "A retinal interface? You're expecting me to use an outdated prototype?"

Lin's look of amusement remained. "It was good enough for field agents a decade ago. It will be good enough for you now."

Fine. I wasn't happy, but I could work with that.

"The Undercity is a psychological prison," Juric said. "It operates without bars or walls, without surveillance or guards. The Algorithm ensures that no one ever truly believes they can escape."

"Do we have operatives sent in ahead of me?" I asked.

He paused.

"What we struggle with..." he paused, "is that its control is so complete that we have, as yet, ever successfully embedded an agent."

I stared at him. Silence settled over the room.

Juric studied me for a moment, then continued. "The system is too effective, Rayne. The moment someone is offloaded, they believe they belong there. Even when we have tried to embed operatives in the past, within weeks... they disappear. They integrate. They forget."

I frowned, feeling the weight of what he was saying.

"You're telling me the ISB has no active assets in the Undercity?"

"None," Lin confirmed. "We can track population densities. We can see shifts in movement. But we have no direct contacts. No field reports. No informants. We are blind."

I sat back in my chair, absorbing the enormity of it. For all the ISB's power… For all the technology and control at its disposal… It had never once successfully penetrated the Undercity. And now I was to go in alone. A slow heat spread in my chest.

I kept my expression neutral, but the weight of Juric's words settled over me like ice.

"No one has ever successfully embedded in the Undercity," he had said. "Not because they were discovered. Not because they were killed. But because they simply forgot their mission."

I leaned forward slightly, my hands pressed against the cold steel table. "You're telling me that trained ISB operatives, men and women with psychological conditioning, with years of preparation, just… 'forget' their mission?"

Juric met my gaze, his expression unreadable. "We've reviewed every attempt. The pattern is always the same. Within weeks, they stop reporting in. And when we send in retrieval squads, they don't resist capture. They don't even remember who they were. Eventually, we have to let them stay. They believe they must."

A slow, insidious chill spread through my chest. It was impossible. I had always known the Undercity was designed to be inescapable—an invisible prison, not of walls and fences, but of the mind. A place where the offloaded never tried to leave because they believed there was nowhere else to go. This meant that the Algorithm wasn't just suppressing movement. It was rewiring people.

I clenched my jaw.

"How?" I demanded. "How is it doing this?"

Juric exchanged a glance with Lin, the Chief Tech Officer. She was the one who answered.

"The Algorithm operates on multiple levels of social conditioning and neurological interface," she said, her tone cool and clinical. "It doesn't just track movement and behavior. It monitors neurological responses. Subconsciously reinforcing compliance through adaptive feedback loops."

I narrowed my eyes. "Whoa! Slow down professor. Explain."

She tapped the display, and a new diagram appeared—a mapped interface of the human brain, overlaid with the Algorithm's influence zones.

"The moment someone is offloaded," she continued, "the system begins a process of psychological Recalibration Through constant environmental stimuli, targeted deprivation, and subliminal reinforcement, the brain is guided into a new reality. A new set of truths. Over time, the neural pathways governing identity, ambition, even memory itself, are overwritten."

I exhaled sharply. I had read about behavioral reinforcement models in training, but I had never imagined something this absolute. I pointed to the diagram. "This is more than conditioning. It's mind control."

Lin rolled her eyes. "If you want to be dramatic, sure."

I ignored the jab. "Then why haven't we used this tech on the upper districts? To prevent offloading altogether?"

"Because it isn't necessary." She leaned back slightly, folding her arms. "In New Columbia, citizens operate on incentives—status, wealth, social approval. The Algorithm rewards them for their obedience and in general, people want that. But in the Undercity? There is nothing to aspire to. Nothing to fight for. No way out. The brain resolves cognitive dissonance the only way it can—by accepting that this is where they want to be. Where they belong."

I clenched my fists beneath the table. That was why no mole had ever lasted. Because the Undercity didn't need guards. It didn't need fences. The prisoners built their own cages.

"And what's your plan for me?" I asked. "How do we prevent it from happening to me?"

Lin looked like she had been waiting for this question. She tapped the console, and a new set of schematics appeared. "This," she said, "is how we keep you from becoming one of them."

I studied the three-tiered approach they had designed to keep my mind intact. The first of which was a Neurochemical Resistance Implant, NRI, a timed micro-dosage of counteractive neurotransmitters injected directly into my bloodstream through a sub-dermal implant. This regulates dopamine, serotonin, and nor-epinephrine to prevent emotional desensitization.

"The offloaded experience a slow suppression of cognitive drive," Lin explained. "The brain stops associating resistance with survival. This implant ensures you maintain motivational, critical thinking, and—most importantly—a desire to leave."

The second consisted of a Sensory Anchor Protocol, a sequence of controlled stimuli embedded in my retinal HUD that was to create flashes of light, coded messages, even sound cues designed to prevent neurological drift. Every six hours, an automated 'reality check' will remind me of who I am.

"Reinforcement is key," Lin said. "The Algorithm works by removing patterns. We counter it by introducing them. You'll get reminders in the form of audio cues, personal data, even scent triggers embedded in your clothing fibers. Every few hours, something will pull you back. And finally, we have developed an Emergency Recall Sequence a pre-recorded 'fail-safe' message to yourself."

"Because the first two may not work?" I tried to sound like I was making a joke, but somewhere in the back of my mind, it is exactly what I was thinking

Lin didn't see it as a joke either "Precisely, it will be stored in your hidden retinal interface and activated only if certain cognitive markers indicate assimilation. You'll make the recording before insertion, If you start to forget, you will remind yourself."

I nodded. I pressed my lips together, then spoke carefully.

"If this technology exists," I said, "why don't we use it to… correct the offloaded?"

Lin and Juric exchanged a glance.

Juric spoke. "Because it's not about whether we can, Rayne," he said. "It's about whether we should."

I frowned.

"New Columbia is built on natural selection," he continued. "Those who fail to maintain their SES—fail to prove their worth—are not meant to return. The Algorithm does not make mistakes. We do not interfere with its judgment."

I looked down for a moment, considering this. We had the tools to reverse offloading. But we chose not to. For the first time in my career, the cold logic of New Columbia felt… fragile. I inhaled sharply, locking away the thought. Now wasn't the time.

I nodded sharply. "Well, what are we waiting for?"

Chapter 14

CAPT. RAYNE - OFFLOADED

I was offloaded the next morning. I thought of the fate of Marla Sedgewick briefly. Maybe she was better off not to have made it here. This place was a fair description of hell.

"Now what?" I wondered. "How do the offloaded know what to do or where to go?

And it struck me immediately. They don't. After my release, I kept my head down and began to walk. Small steps. Nothing that would draw attention. I needed to get away from the front gates. More offloaded were arriving behind me. Confused, pushing, as lost as I was. I needed to find a safe place and figured it wouldn't be anywhere near here, so I pushed deeper into the darkened corridors and tunnels which laid out before me like a maze. The Undercity pressed in. Crowds shifting, bartering, eyes flicking toward me, then away. The smell of burnt plastic and the stench of humans living to closely together hung in the thick hot air. I stumbled my way through the crowd taking it all in. Makeshift living places made from cardboard and broken scraps of wood, plastic signs and torn tarps. I passed places that had obviously been designated as toilet areas, and the smell let me know that sewer systems wasn't a model of efficiency down here.

Around another corner a water line was broken and a spray of cold water cascaded into the narrow alley. A group of women, still wearing their shirts but nothing else, were trying their best to shower. A few men stood close by, facing away.

"Guards for their women" I thought.

The men watched me as I passed by. I tried not to stare but it was hard not to take in the myriads of strangeness, poverty and social interaction of this place.

"You lookin' fer somebody or what?" one of the men grunted.

I ignored him and moved on. Juric's words echoed in my head.

"Your primary objective is reconnaissance. You are not to engage. You are not to make contact unless absolutely necessary."

I made my way deeper inside, past the living quarters and shower stalls to an area which obviously served as a marketplace for this quadrant. God knows how big the Underground is. I assumed there were many markets like this, serving the local population with items of necessity or maybe distractions to help them survive this bleak existence. This market tunnel pulsed with low chatter, the crackle of oil-drum fires, the murmur of trades made in half-lit corners. The place was a hive of barter and desperation. A place in the Undercity where food, medicine, and black-market tech were exchanged.

The market stretched beneath the ruins of an old transit hub, its ceiling a patchwork of rusted beams and repurposed metal sheets, barely holding back the filth-streaked rain that dripped through in slow, lazy plinks. Dim, buzzing lights flickered overhead, throwing uneven shadows across the cracked pavement, their glow barely strong enough to cut through the gloom. Stalls had been cobbled together from whatever scraps could be salvaged—shipping crates, broken shelving, the twisted remains of old storefront awnings. Some had tarps stretched overhead, stained with years of grease and smoke, while others were left open-air, vendors standing in the damp, shrouded in layers of patched and filthy clothing.

The vendor in front of me had sharp, calculating eyes, half-hidden beneath the brim of a scavenged military cap, the fabric so worn it was impossible to tell what color it had once been. His coat was a size too big, cinched at the waist with a strip of fabric that might have been a belt in another life. His hands were dark with oil and grime, his nails chipped, fingertips calloused from years of handling circuitry and scrap metal. His stall was an organized mess—rows of salvaged tech stacked in careful chaos, old monitors flickering with distorted images, circuit boards piled like shuffled playing cards, tangled wires coiled like dead snakes. A single lantern burned low, its yellow glow casting jagged shadows against the rough stone behind him.

The air reeked of burnt plastic and the metallic tang of ozone, the unmistakable scent of fried wiring.

Somewhere nearby, the sizzle of cooking meat and the sharp bite of something pickled cut through the acrid stench, a reminder that hunger and desperation went hand in hand here. Above the murmuring crowd, deal-making voices rose and fell like a tide—some smooth, some sharp, some barely more than words exchanged under breath. The occasional shout of an argument, the slap of something heavy hitting the ground, the click and whir of bootlegged security devices sparking to life. The vendor studied me, expression unreadable. Not unfriendly, but not exactly welcoming either. Just another player in a place where everyone had something to sell and everything had a price.

Rezik moved through the market, his stride lazy, his eyes sharp, studying the stalls with the cold detachment of a man who believed everything in his line of sight already belonged to him. His men flanked him—three of them, built from muscle and bad habits, their eyes flicking over the vendors like they were weighing livestock. They spread out subtly, picking through tables, running their fingers over goods, turning over stolen trinkets and scavenged bits of tech gear as if they had the right to inspect them. No one challenged them. They didn't need to. The weight of Rezik's presence alone was enough to keep the vendors quiet, their backs just a little straighter, their eyes a little lower. He wasn't just here to buy. He was here to remind them. This was his market. His territory.

A young vendor—barely more than a kid, thin and jittery—stood frozen as one of Rezik's men picked through a crate of smuggled protein bars. The thug plucked one out, turning it in his hands before grabbing another, and another, stuffing them into his pockets like he was owed them. The vendor didn't protest, barely even breathed. A few stalls down, an older woman flinched as Rezik himself ran a hand over her wares—worn fabrics, repurposed clothing, patches carefully stitched, into neat piles. Rezik picked one up, studied the threading, and then dropped it back onto the pile like it was nothing. A silent judgment. A verdict on whether she would be allowed to keep selling tomorrow.

He didn't care what was being sold. Only that he had a cut. Any vendor caught trading without his approval, selling something he hadn't sanctioned, keeping a sliver of profit that hadn't crossed his hands first—wouldn't be selling anything in the morning.

Rezik's men continued their quiet sweep, checking for signs of disobedience, of defiance, of vendors who thought they could slip something past him. But Rezik wasn't looking at the stalls anymore.

He was scanning the crowd. Hunting.

I saw him before he saw me. It wasn't hard. Men like him always stood out. He moved like an enforcer— shoulders squared, gaze sweeping for weakness, the weight of entitlement still clinging to him like a scent. He moved through the chaos like a man who had something to prove. But what had caught my attention was the fact that he looked too green, too clean. His coat untattered, his boots barely worn. He had to have been newly offloaded. Fresh from New Columbia's false promises. Now finding a way to regain some sense of power.

Here, there were no uniforms, no rank, no corporate protections. Just predators and prey. I decided to move on. I kept my steps even, purposeful. Just another offloaded nobody trying to navigate the filth.

I had spent years reading people. Watching them. Controlling them. Rezik was easy. A man who feared being invisible. I had to cut through a pair of tables to get some distance between us, but I realized it was too late, he had seen me. When I glanced over my shoulders, his eyes locked mine. Predatory. Calculating. I saw his lips curl like he had just found his next meal. I wasn't afraid of guys like Rezik who thought their brawn could take what they wanted. They saw women as weak, subservient. He walked towards me like I had no option but to give in to him. And that's exactly what makes me dangerous to idiots like him.

"Lost, sweetheart?"

He stepped up to face me, blocking my path between the stalls. Too close. Too familiar. The vendor at the table looked up. Wanting to watch the show. I tried to look humble, but to be honest, I don't have a lot of practice at that. Rezik Vance stood before me, all swagger and arrogance. He grinned, teeth flashing in the dim tunnel light. I immediately knew he'd had a high enough score recently to get good dental work. Most people here did not have such white teeth.

"I haven't seen you around, darling" he said his

eyes scanning my body like I was on the menu. "I like fresh meat" he drooled obscenely. "Fresh meat means nobody's laid claim to you yet, have they?"

I flashed a demur look, my eyes darting between him and his goons.

"I - I'm not sure what -"

Reziks teeth glowed even brighter as his smile showed more teeth. "You don't have any protection" he said, tilting his head. "And that makes you fair game."

He let the back of his hand slide down my cheek. My heart hammered against my ribs. Not from fear. From calculation.

"You are not to engage. You are not to make contact unless absolutely necessary."

The moment his dirty hand touched my face; I made the call - This is necessary. I let my eyes dart, feigning panic, letting him think I was prey. Then I ran.

Obviously, I didn't get far. There wasn't a lot of room between the tables. I made it past a few stalls before one of Rezik's bozos—a thick-necked brute with dull eyes—cut me off, his grip closing around my shoulders like steel. I feigned resistance, twisted, fought, pulled—knowing he'd keep a tight grip. After all, he thought he was stronger than I. And that I was nothing more than a helpless office clerk.

I gasped as another grabbed me from behind, his forearm locking tight around my throat. The chokehold was sloppy—too high, too tight. He didn't know what he was doing. I could have broken free easily. Could have ended this in seconds. But I let my body go limp. Submitting. I let my face drop in defeat. Rezik sauntered up, slow and easy. He stopped just inches from me, tilting his head, studying me like a cat studying a wounded bird. I kept my breath shallow, uneven. A little fear in my eyes. Enough to make him think he had control. Because that's what men like him wanted. Not just to win. But to be seen winning.

"Look at this one," he smiled to the others, voice full of mock amusement. "New. Pretty... and feisty".

I let my muscles slacken just a little more. His hand brushed my chin again. Testing to see what I'd do. And that is when I decided to give them a little demonstration of my own.

I struck fast.

I snapped my head back suddenly— skull colliding with the face of the man holding me. Cartilage crunched. He let out a garbled howl as blood gushed from his shattered nose. I spun, using his staggering weight against him. My knee drove up into his groin—hard. He collapsed. One down. I turned—but the others were already moving. Arms closed around me, pinning me before I could strike again. I decided it was enough class for one day and submitted.

Rezik stepped forward, his grin wider now. "Well, well, well," he said, voice smooth. "We have ourselves a real fighter here, don't we boys?"

I forced myself to breathe fast. Let my body tremble slightly. He wanted a reaction. I gave him one that fit the part.

"Where'd you learn to fight like that, sweetheart?" he said, grinning nastily into my face, eyes wide with excitement.

"I took a course," I said, allowing him to see the confidence in my face.

Rezik chuckled. "Took a course, huh?" His hand pulling away from my face. "Gotta say, you did better than most. You hurt one of my guys." He stepped closer, lowering his voice. "And I like that."

Rezik studied me closer.

"You want to survive here?" he asked.

I stayed silent.

"O.K. Tell you what. I won't hurt you. But you still need protection," he said. "And I'll give it to you. You just have to swear loyalty to me. I could use a strong arm like you. Most guys wouldn't expect it from a little girl like you. Izaak over there certainly didn't."

The words hung between us. I looked at Izaak, blood covered face, still doubled over hands pinned between his legs. I forced myself to hesitate. To look uncertain. This was the opening I needed. Power came with connections. And if I was going to find the rebels here, I needed someone with reach.

I let my shoulders slump slightly. Swallowed. Then, finally—I nodded.

"Alright," I murmured. "Boss..." Then I leaned into and whispered into the side of his face so the others would not hear me "Touch me again and I'll show you what I learned in the second course."

Rezik's dirty little smile suddenly dropped away and his face paled, indicating he clearly understood the threat. Then slowly his toothy, dental ad of a smile reappeared.

"Smart girl." He said stepping back from me. His men released me. I rubbed my wrists where they had held me, then glanced up at him. Rezik's grin was pure satisfaction.

"Welcome to the Undercity, sweetheart."

True to his word, Rezik kept his promise not to touch me. And it didn't take long for me to see that Rezik wasn't interested in me sexually, or any other women, for that matter. I was assigned to protect the new female offloads that he decided needed protection. Young, beautiful and unable to defend themselves, they usually welcomed their fate. "Protection" meant they had food and were safe from violent offenders. In return, they were required to "accompany" some of the more powerful members of this make-shift society. I knew what these poor girls were expected to do, and understood I was here for something bigger. I did my job. No-one touched these girls...unless they could afford the price.

The Undercity never truly slept. The glow of barrel fires flickered against crumbling concrete, casting long shadows over the tunnel walls. Somewhere in the distance, a scuffle broke out—angry voices, a grunt of pain, then silence. But here, near the edge of Rezik's territory, it was quiet. I stepped outside the sleeping quarters, inhaling the stale, metallic air. The market had long since wound down, but the acrid scent of burnt wiring and unwashed bodies still clung to everything.

And then I noticed her.

Sitting in front of the entrance, knees drawn to her chest, arms wrapped around her legs. She didn't look at me. Didn't acknowledge my presence at all. She just stared into the distance; her dark eyes unreadable. I hesitated. Rezik's crew saw the offloaded as currency. As resources to control. Even I had played along, pretending to be just another cog in the Undercity machine. But sitting there, silent, unmoving, barely more than a shadow against the wall… She didn't look like a failed citizen. She looked like someone who had been stolen. And something in me cracked.

I walked over, lowering myself to sit beside her. She didn't flinch. Didn't shift. Didn't react. For a long time, we just sat there, both of us watching the dark. Then I spoke.

"You OK?"

A long pause.

Then, finally, she spoke—soft, quiet, emotionless.

"Yeah, I'm fine."

I looked closer at her. Her hair stuck to her face where the tears had been.

"Doesn't look like you're fine."

She let out a slow, measured breath. Then her eyes rose to mine, something close to hatred, clearly full of anger.

"What do you care? Caring too much down here can get you killed."

The words sent a slow chill down my spine. She turned away, then turned back again to face me.

"Besides, by tomorrow, you'll just sell me off to

the highest bidder and forget I was ever here, won't you?" she asked.

I didn't answer. Because she wasn't wrong. Her gaze drifted back toward the tunnel.

"I wasn't supposed to be here," she said, her voice flat.

None of them were. But I let her speak.

"I had a good score," she continued. "Not high, but… steady. I followed the rules. I worked hard. I never questioned anything."

A bitter laugh—quiet, hollow. "And then one day, that wasn't enough."

She ran a hand over her arms, as if trying to rub something away.

"I got a notice," she said. "A formal invitation to… 'contribute.'"

She didn't need to explain. I already knew. Even in the ISB, we had heard rumors of it. The unspoken expectations of the elite. How they could make an offer—one you weren't allowed to refuse. I felt something tighten in my chest.

"You said no."

She nodded.

I knew the rest. She had said no and just like that, her SES had plummeted. Not because she had broken any laws. Not because she had failed as a citizen. But because one man had decided her fate.

"I started to file an appeal," she said. "but I received a notice that my appeal had been denied before I had even submitted it."

I shifted uneasily. The system had always been

designed to cull the weak. To reward loyalty. But this? This wasn't failure. This was punishment. She turned toward me again.

"You ever wonder how many of us are down here because someone just said we did something wrong?"

I didn't answer. I didn't have to. Her smile was small. Bitter.

"The system is not about failure," she murmured. "It's about obeying, reminding everyone else what happens if you stop obeying."

I had spent my life enforcing the system. Tracking deviations. Offloading the unworthy. I had told myself it was necessary. That the Algorithm was pure. Absolute. But sitting here, beside this girl with a shattered future, in a world where no one was meant to escape… For the first time, I wondered if we were the real failures.

"What's your name?" I asked.

She hesitated.

Then, softly—"Alina."

I nodded. And for the first time since arriving, I told the truth. "I'm Evelyn."

And then something happened. It started with a pulse. Soft, rhythmic—a Recalibration sequence buried beneath my skin. Then the Retinal HUD flickered, a barely perceptible flash of blue filtering through my vision. A voice—familiar, artificial—buzzed in my ear.

"Cognitive drift detected. Reinforcing anchor points."

The flash was brief—just a flicker—but enough to

jolt me back. Lin's protocols had been implanted for this exact reason—to keep my mind from slipping. I gasped for air, struggling against my feelings. I suddenly remembered who I was.

I wasn't one of them. I wasn't offloaded. I was Evelyn Rayne. A top Enforcer, Captain of the ISB. A guardian of the Algorithm's will. This world—this filth-ridden cesspool of failures and degenerates—was not mine. It was trying to assimilate me.

And Alina?

Obviously a plant, a lie looking to draw me in. Hoping to find a weakness in me. She was a reminder of why New Columbia had to be protected. Juric's voice echoed in my memory.

"The Undercity is designed to lure you in. It will tempt you with its stories, with its suffering. It will try to make you believe these people are victims."

Lin had been more blunt.

"The second you start empathizing, you've already lost. You are there to observe, infiltrate, destroy. If you start thinking like them, you'll become them. And the Algorithm does not tolerate corruption."

Struggling to my feet, I stumbled away, trying to catch my breath, regain my senses. I had trained for this. I had been equipped for this. And yet—they almost got me there. I swallowed hard. Because for a fraction of a second, I had forgotten what Alina was. I had almost seen her as a person. Alina glanced up, her expression unreadable. For a moment, I almost reached out. Almost asked her something else. But I didn't. Instead, I turned away, forcing myself to reset.

This was a mission. A necessary infiltration. Alina was not my concern. The rebels were. I turned away, eyes sharp, focus restored. I needed to keep searching, to find them. To break them. I would complete my assignment. And then, I could return to where I belonged. To perfection. To order. To the only world that made sense.

"But damn! They almost got me there."

Chapter 15

SECTRET LIFE OF SMUGGLERS

As an enforcer myself, it didn't take me long in the Undercity to understand one thing—no one survived without a hand to pull them up or a boot to keep them down. And Rezik Vance? He was still trying to get the boot off his back. He carried himself like a man who ruled these streets, but every low-level enforcer in this place could see he was just another small-time predator, scraping together whatever power he could. But power—real power—came from connections. And I needed to know who his connections were.

Rezik's sudden disappearance had caught my attention. Once a week, sometimes more, he'd slip away without a word, only to return with contraband tech—valuable, clean, and unmistakably from New Columbia. I had expected a smuggling ring, maybe a network of bribes keeping a supply chain alive. But men like Rezik didn't operate alone. Someone was feeding him. And whoever that was? They were my next step up the chain.

The Undercity was built like a trap—layers of filth and forgotten corridors, dead ends disguised as pathways, entrances that led nowhere. If you didn't know your way, you disappeared. But Rezik did. So, when he slipped away that night, so did I. He moved like a man trying not to be followed, his route winding, erratic. Through the back alleys of the market. Past rows of scavenged goods and hungry-eyed vendors. Down a passage behind a collapsed water main. I stayed just far enough behind, pressing myself into the shadows when he hesitated. He never looked back.

Rezik slipped through a metal door, barely wide enough for a man to pass through. I waited. Counted to thirty. Then I followed. The tunnel beyond was silent, the air cooler, untouched by the constant stink of the Market. And then I heard it. A voice. Smooth. Confident. Amused. I crouched behind a rusted-out bulkhead, peering through a jagged hole in the metal. Rezik stood inside a dimly lit space, not much larger than a storage room. The walls were lined with crates—the type he often returned with. But it wasn't the contraband that held my attention. It was the man with him.

He was polished. Controlled. Well-fed. Well-dressed. Well-groomed. Everything the Undercity was not. And Rezik? Rezik looked at him like a starving man looks at salvation. The stranger stepped closer, reaching out with a slow, deliberate motion. His fingers brushed against Rezik's jaw; a touch so intimate it almost didn't belong in a place like this. Rezik paused for a moment. Then, abandoning all hesitation, he leaned in. And kissed him.

A dozen scenarios had played out in my mind when I followed Rezik. None of them had been this. This was no longer a low tier smuggling operation.

This wasn't just another hidden meeting between petty criminals. This was something much more dangerous. Because in the Undercity, relationships like this could be fatal. Something Rezik would not want to have others discover, I was certain. And for me? It was leverage.

I retraced my steps, moving carefully, silently. By the time I slipped back into the section I now called home, the fires had burned lower, the night settling into uneasy stillness. I waited. And when Rezik returned at dawn, he was carrying a crate—the same as always. Routers. Storage devices. Hard drives. He set it down with a grunt, wiping sweat from his brow.

I didn't say a word. Because I had a decision to make. I could blackmail him. Break him. Destroy his hold over this place. Or I could use him. Because it was obvious that whoever his well-connected, well-fed lover was—he was part of tech supply chain, and the rebels needed tech.

I decided that instead of going after Rezik I would move up a rung in the ladder. I'd get in with the supplier. And to get to him, I just had to get Rezik to back me. And I knew that would be extremely easy to do. Because Rezik had a goddamn ego. That was the thing about men like him. They weren't satisfied with simple survival. They wanted power. They wanted to be feared, respected. They wanted others to pretend that the Undercity hadn't already swallowed them whole. And I was about to give him exactly what he wanted.

Or at least, let him believe I would.

It was late, our vendor's stall thick with the smell of stale beer, and damp concrete. The other goons had drifted off, leaving Rezik slouched in a makeshift chair, boots propped up on a crate, drinking from a dented metal flask. I chose my moment. I approached him slowly, deliberate, just enough sway in my stance to make him take note. He glanced up, half-lidded eyes glinting in the dim light.

"What do you want, sweetheart?"

I smiled. Sweet, nonthreatening. Just another low-level girl trying to carve out a sliver of safety in a world ruled by men like him. But Rezik wasn't a predator tonight. Tonight, I was the predator.

"Look, Rezik" I said softly "I've been watching your operation. And I want to help you."

He laughed, tipping his flask back.

"That so?" He wiped his mouth with the back of his hand. "And what exactly makes you think I need help?"

I tilted my head.

"Because you're playing small."

The amusement in his expression flickered. I took another step closer, lowering my voice.

"Look at you," I said. "Running this little slum, scraping by, selling routers and secondhand storage like a petty street vendor. And we both know that's not what you want, is it?"

His jaw tightened.

"Careful, sweetheart." His eyes narrowed.

But he didn't tell me to stop.

"You had power in New Columbia, didn't you?" I

said, hinting that I knew more than I did. I was circling slowly, keeping my voice low, like I was letting him in on a secret. "You were someone. But now?" I gestured around us, to the filth, the stench, the desperation.

"You think running a little tech hustle is enough?" I let a scoff slip into my voice. "You think selling a few stolen hard drives is ever going to make you a king down here?"

His fingers twitched around the flask. I was getting under his skin. I pressed deeper.

"You know why New Columbia works, Rezik? Why do Callus and his Board thrive? Because they understand what you seem to have forgotten—power is taken. Strength is earned. And now?"

I let my lips curl in something almost mocking.

"You're just another failed player. A warlord in a gutter."

Rezik's nostrils flared, his grip on the flask turning white-knuckled. For a second, I thought he might lunge at me, wrap those hands around my throat just to prove he could. I held his gaze. Waited. And then—

He grinned.

"You've sure got some balls lady," he muttered.

"I have ambition." I leaned in again, dropping my voice to a whisper. "Think bigger, Rezik."

"I've been down here a couple months, and I already own the tech supply in this sector." he countered. I have plans to take over a couple more."

Rezik had a habit of thinking with his ego first. I was counting on that. He saw himself as a rising power in the Undercity, but the truth was—he was just another bottom-feeder, scraping what he could before a bigger fish showed up to swallow him. I was hoping to feed into that insecurity. I wanted to make sure he saw my offer as his one chance to climb higher.

"No, you run a scrap yard," I said, keeping my tone tight, taunting him. "I'm talking real tech. Secure comm units. Data-masking hardware. The kind of gear that moves fast and the right buyers will pay big money to get their hands on."

His demeanor faltered, just for a second. He scoffed, masking it with arrogance.

"You think I wouldn't love to get my hands on those?" He took a slow sip from his flask. "You got the money to pay for that stuff? Gotta have it upfront too, not promises of later return. And even if you did have the cash, where are you going to find them? You think they just leave that stuff laying around?"

"Not down here," I admitted. "But they do up there."

That got his attention. I let the words settle, my expression unreadable.

"I have a connection," I lied. "Someone with access in the security sector. They overbuy, stockpile, use up budgets so they won't see cuts in the next cycle. I can get them if I can get to her. But I can't get to her from down here."

Rezik tilted his head, suspicious now. "Who? What exactly are you asking for?"

I hesitated—just enough hesitation to make it feel real.

"A way back to the surface. Just for a short time."

Rezik laughed, shaking his head. "That's suicide. Even if you somehow made it topside, you'd be flagged in seconds. Drones would fry you before you could blink."

"I know," I agreed easily. "That's why I need cover—just enough to get in, make the arrangements, and get out."

He was still watching me, still skeptical. I leaned in slightly, pushing him toward the decision.

"You ever been rich before, Rezik?"

He didn't answer. He didn't have to.

"I don't mean black-market-rich," I pressed. "I mean real power. No hiding in the shadows. No scrounging for scraps. No more pretending you're something bigger than you are." I leaned hard on the word 'pretending'.

His jaw tightened. He wanted it. I just had to give him the right excuse.

"You're full of shit!" he scowled waving a hand at me.

"Look," I said, lowering my voice just enough to make it feel like a confession. "You think I really learned self-defense and fighting from watching how-to videos? How's Izaak's nose? Has the swelling gone down any?"

I let him put two and two together. A simple office drone, innocent and sweet little Ms. Sedgewick beating the crap out of one his guys? Making offers to supply illegal and highly sought after contraband? I could see the cogs turning in his head as the realization that I may be more than he expected spread though his thick skull. I kept the pressure on.

"I was upper tier. SES 5.8. Financial Division," I lied.

Rezik narrowed his eyes. Suspicion was his best ally. He pressed me on it.

"Bullshit."

I let out a slow breath, like I was debating whether to keep going. "I worked under a manager who oversaw SES point allocation for corporate promotions. His job was to approve increases, make sure everything was running clean."

I paused, then added "Except it wasn't."

I could see the shift in his posture, the interest just barely outweighing his doubt.

"What? Skimming the finances?"

"Not skimming money. Reallocating SES scores. The money came after." I let the words sink in before continuing.

"See, most people assume the Algorithm controls everything. But for high-level executives— there are still approvals that had to be made manually. And my boss?" I chuckled bitterly. "He figured out a way to make extra SES off them."

"Whoa! How'd he manage that?" Rezik said, amazed. He was buying it.

Gotcha!

I kept going.

"See, the thing about SES scores?" I said watching Rezik's expression carefully. "They fluctuate all the time. A hundredth of a point here, a thousandth of a point there—most people don't think about it because we only care about the tenths. But the Algorithm does. And my boss?" I tightened my face, squinting slightly. "He thought about it too."

Rezik leaned forward, flask forgotten in his hand. Bewilderment spread across his face. I made the math easier for him.

"The system calculates SES based on a ton of your actions, right?" I continued. "It totals the score and then performs a weighted calculation. A very precise number. Its very rare that the calculation comes out as a nice, neat number. What if a person's exact score is 3.5077? He's a 3.5, right? But where does the .0077 go? I paused. "It doesn't just vanish. The Algorithm doesn't err, remember?"

Rezik's eyes narrowed. "So? What good is 77 thousandths of a point?

"There are millions of records. What if you could mangage siphon off just 1,000 of them?" I asked, then chided him with the answer.

"I'll give you a hint. You suddenly have 7.7 points to sell."

Reziks eyes widened. "He was siphoning them off?"

I nodded.

"He funneled those fractions of a point into a bogus slush account—a reserve of credit balance adjustments. The kind of thing that shouldn't really exist but does, because somewhere, the math has to balance. And if you have the right clearance, you get to make minor credit decisions outside the Algorithm. It's the "human control" factor Callus likes to brag about. Only in this case, it's the "Human Corruption" factor."

I let the silence settle for a moment, watching the gears turn in his head before dropping the final piece.

"Once word got out to the right folks that he had some under-the-table credits he was willing to let go of, he suddenly became very, very popular."

"Now, who do you suppose would want to buy SES points?" I said in a falsetto voice of feigned innocence.

Rezik grunted knowingly. "Uh, everyone ... anyone with any money that is."

"Exactly. Executives whose security clearance was about to dip below 6.0. Corporate officers angling for a promotion. Someone a little nervous about an upcoming review and just wanted a tiny boost as insurance."

I spread my hands, fanning them out at the imagined riches.

"Fancy cars. A yacht. All-expense-paid first-class trips. You name it, he had it. All built on scraps no one even knew were missing."

Rezik let the flask down slowly, his jaw open, eyeing the images I just drew for him. Suddenly he snapped out of it.

"And then he found out that you found out."

I raised my hands in defeat. "Yep, and, well, here I am."

Rezik was looking at me differently now. This was insider information. Something I shouldn't know. Something only someone who had been in the upper tiers would know. And that was the key. I wasn't asking him to believe a story. I was giving ideas, and he was building his own story, and believing it.

"The only reason I caught on," I continued, "was because one of my coworkers got flagged for a review. His score dropped a point and half. The next day, his boss—who hadn't done a damn thing in five years—coincidentally went up by two."

I shook my head.

"Curious, I ran an audit. My boss was so lazy, he often had me run financial deposits under his name. He gave me his access so he could go golfing while I filed reports. I just followed the paper trail. It was airtight—almost. Just enough anomalies to see a pattern. Stupid me, when I opened a file, I didn't realize I triggered a two-party verification. He flagged it as a breach and I suddenly I was looking at an "access denied" code and the screen. And my proof? Vanished. Next day my SES dropped. 1.8. I was offloaded that very day."

Rezik exhaled through his nose, looking at me with something new in his eyes. Belief. Greed. A man seeing opportunity.

I leaned into him, making my face as hard and tight as I could. "I want back in, Rezik. Not for the money. I don't give a damn about money. I want revenge. I want that son-of-a-bitch to pay for what he did to me. I want him to have to live down here too. If that means giving you access to some high-tech schoolboy gadgets, then so be it. I can make that happen. But I need you to get me there so I can take that miserable bastard out."

I could see the wheels turning in his head.

This wasn't just some girl looking for an escape. This was a ticket to a whole new ballgame. And I had just handed it to him free of charge. Rezik took another swig from his flask, then let out a slow breath.

"You're asking for a lot, sweetheart."

"I know."

He studied me for a long time. Then, finally, he nodded. "I might be able to work something. I'll introduce you to my guy."

"That's all I ask."

He chuckled under his breath.

"You better hope you're not full of shit," he murmured.

Chapter 16

IRIS AND ADAM PLOT

The room was dim, lit only by the soft glow of outdated monitors and flickering data streams—a patchwork of salvaged tech, hidden in the deepest layers of the Undercity. But despite the rough setup, I felt that this was now the most powerful room in New Columbia. More powerful than any story I'd worked on at the Truth. Here, we weren't just discussing rebellion. We were about to rewrite the untruths the System called reality.

Adam sat across from me, his face lit by the screens, casting shadows and highlights on his face. I suddenly saw just how handsome he was. The sharp angles of his face carried the weight of experience, a quiet confidence etched into the lines at the corners of his mouth. His silver-streaked hair, neatly kept, gave him an air of distinction—someone who had once belonged in boardrooms but had learned to survive in shadows. His gray eyes were piercing yet measured, always watching, always calculating, weighing everything before taking action. There was strength in his stance, not the exaggerated kind born from vanity, but the quiet resilience of a man who had endured, adapted, and refused to break.

I drew his attention to the raw data spread across the terminal. A goldmine of information. Files that proved the Oligarchs had been manipulating the Algorithm—not just bending it to their will, but actively rewriting truth itself.

"Alright," I said, tapping a finger against the console. "We have our evidence. Now, how do we expose it without getting shut down in seconds?"

Adam leaned back in his chair, still studying the figures. "We'll have to make it look like its coming from within the System, not an outside feed. It needs to be found organically."

"Convince the system that it has uncovered the problem?" I asked.

"Right. We slowly feed the information in, in staggered, calculated releases," he said, deep in concentration. "Nothing too obvious. Just… irregularities. Enough to trigger a review but not enough to set off alarms which would lead to a full lock down."

I nodded slowly. "What if the information made it into some kind of regular review, a weekly financial report or balance report? A few small discrepancies. Links to undeleted log or two showing irregularities and unreported transactions. It would look like someone wasn't thorough."

Adam's fingers drummed against the desk. "We make it look like someone was sloppy, didn't completely cover their tracks. We let the system itself detect the errors."

"It won't scream 'conspiracy'" I pressed on, "it just

looks like simple corruption. It will soon discover its much deeper than that."

Adam perked a little, obviously following my logic. "If we can convince the system that there are discrepancies, it won't dismiss them external attacks since the investigation itself was internal. The Truth loves exposing 'bad actors'—as long as it reinforces the integrity of the system."

"These guys are good at covering their tracks. They're careful. The don't screw up" I said. "So we screw up for them. We make the mistakes they thought they didn't. We let the Algorithm find it and they'll start blaming each other for making rookie mistakes."

Adam exhaled, impressed.

"Not bad, Delacroix."

I winked. "Not done yet. We start doing it again, and again, slightly different each time, but a series of red flags start becoming a pattern of red flags. By the time anyone realizes what's happening, the system itself will have convinced itself that something is happening and start to move on them. Correcting the problem."

"OK", Adam said, sitting forward, "say we get the first wave out, what stops the Board themselves from declaring it a cyberattack? If they label it a breach, they'll have the justification to purge everything and tighten the system."

"We have the actual records, time stamped, valid," I said. "No hacks. No intrusions. Remember, they are actually doing this. Its undeniable."

"An internal investigation still won't go public,

though" Adam countered. "It will identify the problem, sure, maybe even adjust those responsible, but the system won't admit there was ever a problem that high up. 'Security override to protect legitimacy' is the protocol-built in."

"That's a real thing?" I asked, surprised.

"I installed the codes myself" he sighed. "The security of the city relies on the confidence of the people. It won't make the news."

"That's where my reports come in. I'll write the exposé. Report the bad actors. Make it public."

"Well, you'd have to get it past the review process. It will still need to be vetted by the content Algorithms."

"OK, what if we bypass the usual editorial vetting process. We inject the files directly into the 'Approved for Broadcast' category?"

"That's some high-clearance security," Adam said raising his eyebrows in disbelief. "You'd need access to The Truth's content storage."

I gave him a knowing look. "And that'd be where your people come in, wouldn't it?"

Adam chuckled. "Alright. Assume we can do it. What stops the public from dismissing it? The SES elites won't care. The lower ranks already assume corruption. How do we make this hit a nerve?"

"We make it personal," I said.

Adam's brow furrowed.

"The Oligarchs are a unified front supporting Callus' policies—at least, that's what they want people to believe," I explained. "But they're not. They're constantly maneuvering, watching each other for signs of betrayal. If we can inject reports suggesting that one of them is cutting side deals without the others, siphoning power—"

"The others will turn on them," Adam finished, realization dawning.

I nodded. "We manufacture the purge from within. Make them think someone is trying to push Callus into removing the 'unfaithful one.' But they won't know which one is setting them up. They'll start hunting their own, dismantling their own power structure for us."

"You want to create a witch hunt!" Adam let out a slow breath. "Damn. That's…pretty awesome. But also, very risky."

"Riskier than doing nothing? It takes the heat off us by distracting the system allocations that are looking for our deleted records."

He met my gaze, considering. Then he grinned. "I think I like how you think."

"One more thing," Adam said, eyes narrowing. "What happens if they decide to call the bluff, understanding that if one goes down, they all go down. They'll squabble among themselves, sure, but self-protection is stronger than vengeance. Even if it goes public, you know they're never going to be brave enough to do anything."

"Then, we don't worry about what the public thinks." I stated flatly.

He frowned.

"We only have to get Callus himself," I said. "He

is addicted to the news. If we can convince him that there is a plot against him then he'll be the one rooting out traitors. He'll do the work we can't."

Adam's jaw tensed for a moment before he relaxed it again.

"We weaponize Callus' paranoia?"

I nodded. "That was already my plan. I'll write it so it doesn't attack Callus. We reinforce the idea that he's the good guy being betrayed. Once he starts seeing enemies among his own..."

Adam let out a low chuckle. "Kinda like you did with the interview story?"

"Please, —don't remind me."

He ran a hand through his hair, the dim glow of the monitors reflected in his eyes as he processed the information.

I leaned back, feeling a rush of panic as I realized the whole plan depended on one thing. Me. Writing the best damned investigative journalism as if my life depended on it. And it did.

"Now let's see how good my writing really is."

Chapter 17

CAPT. RAYNE'S SECRET

Lucian Vale was not a man who trusted easily. He also didn't like loose ends. Rezik had convinced him to meet with me, some newly offloaded secretary, on the premise that I had something the two of them wanted, Needed.

He sat across from me, fingers idly tracing the rim of a glass filled with something far too expensive to have come from the Undercity. Rezik stood beside him, arms crossed, watching me with that same cocky amusement he always wore—like a kid who had half-figured out a magic trick but still didn't quite understand how it worked.

I had been in the room for less than a minute, and already, I could feel Lucian dissecting me. He had barely spoken since I walked in, but that didn't mean he wasn't studying me. Weighing me. Trying to decide if I was worth the risk. Rezik lounged against the wall, looking smug. He thought this meeting was already won. He didn't understand how carefully someone like Lucian played this game.

"So," Lucian said swirling the ice in his glass with his finger. "You need access to the city. And I'm supposed to just... take your word that helping you is worth the risk?”

He said it lazily, like this was all a waste of his time. But his eyes were sharp. He was testing me. Good. I leaned back slightly, tilting my head as if considering.

“I think you’re misunderstanding something, Lucian. I’m not asking you to help me.”

One brow arched ever so slightly.

“No?”

“No,” I said, my voice light, controlled. “I’m offering to help you.”

Lucian paused, taking a slow sip from his glass. “Oh, I doubt you can do that. You see, I don’t make deals with desperate people looking to help people they barely know. Desperation makes them stupid. And stupid gets them killed.”

Rezik chuckled. “She’s not so stupid. She’s got connections.”

Lucian barely spared him a glance. “She says she does.” His gaze returned to me. “But people say all sorts of things, don’t they?”

I met his eyes, matching his composure, obviously directing the insult back to him. “Yes, they do, don’t they?”

The smallest flicker of amusement. A tiny crack in the mask. But Lucian wore a mask that did not easily crack. That much was clear. His composure was reserved, one leg crossed over the other, eyes watching the cubes in his glass as he swirled it in his hands. I could see he was measuring, calculating the risk I might or might not pose.

“Tell me something, Marla,” Lucian said at last,

his voice smooth, deliberate. "How exactly did you manage to get this far?"

I tilted my head slightly. "I just followed Rezik."

Lucian gave a small, almost patronizing smile. "Cute. But you and I both know that's not what I meant."

I didn't answer.

He leaned forward, resting his elbows on his knees. "You're new to the Undercity. Freshly offloaded. And yet, you haven't fallen into the usual patterns." His eyes flickered, sharp and assessing. "Do you know how rare that is?"

I stayed silent.

"It's a funny thing, the Undercity," Lucian continued. "Most people who come here? They don't fight to leave. Hell, within a few weeks, most of them don't even remember that leaving is an option. It's..." he paused, searching for the right word, "...self-containing."

He watched me carefully, and I knew what he was really saying. I didn't look away.

"And yet here you are," he murmured. "Still thinking about getting out. Still wanting to get back to the world above."

He let the implication settle between us. As if saying "you're not playing be the rules. And that makes you dangerous". I exhaled slowly, feigning reluctance. His statement had hit me hard. How could I be so stupid? I had opened up a hole in my cover, an inconsistency that someone like Lucian would pounce on and dissect until he found the truth. Stupid mistake.

The damn Algorithm—its pull, its suffocating design. Making me lose focus, slipping, letting myself think like one of them? I forced the moment aside, holding that fake mask of controlled hesitation. Then, when I spoke, my voice was calm, deliberate—as if I'd been carefully choosing my words all along.

"I don't give a damn about escape," I said, my voice measured. "I just want revenge."

Lucian raised an eyebrow.

"Revenge?"

I nodded, leaning forward slightly, letting my expression sharpen.

"I know I'm not getting out of here," I admitted. "I know I'll never see the top levels of New Columbia again, never breathe clean air or live under anything but artificial light. I can't fix my SES score. I know all that."

I glanced at Rezik, then back at Lucian.

"But there's a man somewhere who put me here. And the only thing that matters to me now—the only thing—is making sure he joins me."

Lucian studied me, his face unreadable.

I let my voice drop to something colder, more vicious.

"You said it yourself. Most people forget about the world above. But me? I can't forget, because I need him to suffer. Every second, every minute, every waking hour—I think about that bastard sitting in his comfortable office, climbing the SES ladder while I rot down here. And every time I remember that..."

I paused, slowly and deliberately.

"...it keeps me focused. Keeps me from falling into the darkness down here. Because this isn't just my prison, Lucian. It's his future."

Silence.

Lucian's expression was carefully neutral, but I knew I had his attention now.

"So I just hand you a way up there?" Lucian finally said. "That's a big risk for someone I just met."

I tilted my head. "I'm not asking you to hand me anything. Just... give me a window. A crack in the door. Just enough time to reach my contact, arrange the drop, and come back. I'll be caught eventually—the drones will see to that—but I only need a few hours."

His fingers tapped a slow, thoughtful rhythm against the edge of his glass.

"Even if I believed you," he said, "what's my incentive? What stops you from getting up there and then come back empty-handed?"

I turned my gaze to Rezik.

"If I come back empty-handed," I said casually, "do you think our dear friend here will be so... friendly?"

Rezik's grin widened. He liked that answer.

Lucian, however, remained unmoved.

"And if security traces you back, if you—hypothetically—lead them to an entrance that may or may not exist? If they discovered a hidden little secret which may or may not exist..."

His voice trailed off. He was still pretending.

Pretending there wasn't a way out. Pretending he wasn't the one controlling it. But when he used the word "pretending" I saw my move.

"Oh, I agree," I said, shifting the tone ever so slightly. "It's very important to guard secrets down here. In fact, when certain secrets get out into the open, people tend to get hurt."

Lucian's fingers stopped tapping.

Rezik's confidence faltered.

I glanced over to Rezik, driving the knife deeper. "Didn't your boys just give one of the vendors a little trouble because they thought he was a little friendly with his work buddy?"

The tension in the room shifted. Lucian didn't blink. Didn't react. But the air changed. I let my gaze settle on Rezik, holding it just long enough. Then I slowly turned to look at Lucian.

"Some of his thugs are a little... homophobic, I think," I mused, watching Lucian's expression. Then I looked over to Rezik. "That poor bastard was lucky to survive the thrashing they gave him. Think he's going to be alright, Rezik?"

Silence. Lucian sat completely still. Rezik shifted slightly, his expression replaced with something less certain. I turned back to Lucian and smiled, just a little.

"Secrets can be so hard to keep, don't you think?"

I stepped into New Columbia from inside the meat

locker in the back of Earl Ray's BBQ and Butcher shop, in the heart of the Central District. Once I stepped outdoors into the light of day, the drones were on me before my eyes could even adjust to the sunlight.

Chapter 18

CAPT. RAYNE'S RETURN

The drones dropped me unceremoniously in front of ISB Headquarters, their cold, mechanical claws releasing me the moment my feet hit the pristine black marble floor. I barely had time to straighten before two uniformed guards flanked me. Not enforcers. ISB security. They didn't speak, didn't hesitate. They simply turned and expected me to follow. Which I did.

The halls of the ISB were just as I remembered them—immaculate, efficient, and utterly devoid of personality. The polished floors swallowed every footstep, the walls lined with cool steel paneling, broken only by embedded surveillance units tracking every move. The air smelled like filtered sterility, the artificial scent of a place that had never known disorder. A stark contrast to where I had just come from. The guards led me into the heart of the building, through a set of reinforced doors that slid open to reveal the ISB war room. The conference room was wide, circular, and dominated by a massive central table, its smooth surface embedded with holographic projectors that flickered with incoming data streams, security feeds, and encrypted transmissions. Monitors lined the far wall, displaying everything from SES fluctuations to energy consumption rates in various districts. This was the nerve center of control. At the head of this control, waiting for me, was Locke.

Lin and Juric sat on either side of him, hands resting on the table, fingers interlaced, watching me like I had just walked in from the dead.

For a moment, no one spoke. Then Juric let out a low whistle. "Damn, Rayne. You actually made it back."

Lin grinned. "I owe Juric a bottle of scotch now. He said you'd be back."

I narrowed my eyes. "And you bet against me?"

She shrugged. "Look, it wasn't personal. It's statistical. Ten weeks is a long time down there. The mind-trap tends to do its job."

Ten weeks. I hadn't realized how much time had passed. It had felt like a lifetime. I looked at Director Locke.

"Sir? which side did you come down on?"

Locke's expression was blank, his voice was dry. "I didn't bet at all, Captain Rayne. I don't gamble."

He paused. "But if I had, I would have put my money with Lin. Well done, Captain."

I tried to hide the blush of pride such a compliment meant, coming from Locke. I decided not to push my luck and didn't acknowledge it.

"I guess it's good you don't gamble, then. The Director of the ISB giving away bottles of scotch could be somewhat embarrassing."

Locke let out a rare chuckle. "Yes. Good thing."

Lin leaned forward, studying me. "You look..." she

searched for the word, "...better than I expected."

I caught a glimpse of myself in the polished black marble behind Locke. There weren't many mirrors in the Undercity. Not a lot of polished surfaces or reflective glass. Nothing to remind people what they had become. Now, I saw it for the first time in ten weeks. Gaunt. Hollowed out. My cheekbones were sharper, my skin paler, a sickly contrast against the grime smudged along my jaw and throat. Dark circles ringed my eyes, making them look sunken, shadowed. My hair—God, my hair—was tangled, stiff from sweat and recycled air, uneven where I had hacked off a portion to keep it from constantly falling into my face. Dirt had settled into every crevice of my skin, beneath my nails, into the worn seams of my clothing.

And the clothes—what had once been a standard-issue corporate worker's blouse and slacks was now a patchwork of filth and torn fabric, stiff from weeks of wear, stained from alley dust, engine smoke, and whatever the hell else had soaked into them in the Undercity. I put my hand up to my face. If this was better...

I took my eyes away from my reflection and met Lin's gaze again. "Yeah? well... thanks, I think. Not sure what you expected."

"Sure" she said, "It just didn't seem very polite to say you look like hell, which you do."

She was smiling.

"When in Rome" I replied, smiling back.

"So?" Locke finally said, bringing us back to reality. "Let's hear your debriefing. Sit."

Locke's voice was sharp, a command, not an invitation. I lowered myself into the chair, worn down but steady.

"No rank. No formalities. Just you and me right now," he said, leaning forward. "Ten weeks inside. Let's start with something simple. Are you compromised?"

"No," I said firmly. "Cover's solid. They think I'm just another desperate offloaded looking for a way up."

I told them my cover-story that I was looking for revenge, why I still had a desire to get to top in spite of the neurotransmitters trying to defeat me. I told them about Lucian Vale, his connection to Rezik, and the tech smuggling operation. I explained how deep their black market ran, how their network was bigger and better organized than we thought. But I also made it clear—I still wasn't close enough to find out who was leaking data, or where Iris Delacroix had been hidden.

Locke nodded. "Any slip-ups? Anyone watching you?"

I hesitated. My mind flashed back to Lucian Vale's suspicious glare, the way he had studied me.

"One. The tech dealer, Lucian Vale. He doesn't trust me. Smart. Sharp. Not easily manipulated."

"Does he suspect?"

"Not yet. But if I stay up here too long, he will."

Locke filed that away with a sharp nod.

"What about Rezik?" He asked.

"A petty lord of a small-time black-market trade. Thinks he's smarter than he is," I said. "He wants power. That makes him easy to control."

"Good." Locke pressed his fingers together. "Tell

me what we don't know."

"We don't know how close these two are to the rebels. I suspect that Vale and Rezik are tied in to the supply line feeding the rebels the tech they need to operate. But I also suspect they are small time players. However, they're looking for a source of high-end black -market tech products," I said. "Vale wants them. Rezik wants them. I told them I can get it for them."

Lin raised an eyebrow. "Bold."

"If I can get them what they want—demonstrate that I have the connections," I concluded, "I can climb higher. Get us to whoever is leaking data. And, if my hunch is right, where I can find one Iris Delacroix."

Locke thought for a moment. "And what do you suggest?"

"Encryption devices. I think that's the next step," I said.

Locke's expression didn't change. But instead of agreement, he gave a stern refusal.

"We are not supplying the enemy with weapons they can use against us," he said.

I let out a breath - I had expected that. "Then don't think of them as weapons."

Locke gave me his look. His "you'd better make me understand, quickly" look.

"Think of them as bait."

All three of them watched me now. Waiting.

Locke frowned. "You want to bait them with non-working encryption transmitters? He looked frustrated.

"No, functional, but traceable. If we embed them with beacons like the one I have, we will be able to—"

I stopped mid-sentence as my words had caused a ripple in the room. Suddenly, all three of them were shooting side-eye glances at each other. A long, knowing silence stretched between them.

"What. Did I say something funny?" I asked.

Finally, Lin sighed. "Well, about the beacon..." She hesitated, glancing at the others. "Uh... well."

"Lin?" I pressed.

"They kind of, uh, don't work," she admitted.

I stared at her. Blinking. Processing.

"You lost me," I said. She thought I was asking her to explain.

"Well, it's not that simple to break the algorithm's security," she said quickly. "The neurological dampening field in the Undercity—your signal was scrambled the second you went under. We tried to compensate, but..."

I interrupted. "I get that. I mean you literally lost me?"

Lin grimaced, looking to Locke for backup. He gave her none.

"How exactly where you planning to extract me?" I demanded.

Juric cleared his throat. "Ah. Well. That's the thing."

Silence.

I looked between them. They weren't joking.

"You guys aren't instilling much confidence in me right now," I said flatly.

The room fell silent for another minute. Finally, Juric broke the tension. "Hey, come on... water under the bridge, right? We had every confidence in you Evelyn. And look—here you are, safe and sound!"

I stared daggers at him.

"Fine," I snapped. "If beacons are useless, where's that leave us? If I don't return with something in the next few hours, we're going to lose this window of opportunity."

Juric held his hands up in submission. "Hang on, he said, we got you." He tapped the console, and a holographic blueprint flickered to life. "We don't need beacons," he said. "These devices already transmit redundant data. They won't be expecting that."

I leaned in.

"Our encryption hardware has a secondary layer," he explained. "No matter how many times they wipe it, it'll still transmit a ghost key—one we can read."

Lin grinned. "We won't be tracking the devices. They'll be broadcasting their location."

I considered that. "You already anticipated these things ending up on the black market."

"Of course," Juric said. "You think this is the first time someone's wanted to steal high-end security tech?"

Locke had been quiet, listening. Finally, he nodded.

"Get them to her. We need her back down there ASAP."

Locke looked at me, sharp, decisive.

"You have your cover?"

"I do."

"And you're good? Here?" He tapped his middle finger to his temple.

"I am."

Locke leaned forward slightly; his voice lower, quieter. "Then let's get you back down there."

For the first time ever, I saw him smile, a true, natural smile. Holding his nose with one hand, he waved me out with the other.

Chapter 19

THE PAYOFF PAYS OFF

The night swallowed me whole. I left the ISB and moved fast, keeping my head down, my hood up. The streets of New Columbia were never truly empty—watchful eyes lurked everywhere, both human and mechanical. Earl Ray's BBQ & Butcher Shop stood as unassuming as ever, the neon sign flickering faintly against the dark storefront. The scent of smoked meat and grease hung in the air, masking the decay of the Central District. I slipped into the alley, pressing my back against the cool brick, listening. The coast was clear.

The back door's lock was a joke. A small, thin blade between the frame and latch, a careful flick of my wrist, and I was inside. The warmth and stench of raw meat hit me first. I moved past hanging cuts of pork and beef, stepping carefully. The meat freezer was just ahead. I pulled open the heavy steel door and slipped inside, closing it behind me. Cold. Silent.

I counted three paces forward, then reached behind the stacked crates. My fingers found the seam. A hidden latch clicked beneath my grip, and a panel in the floor creaked open. I exhaled sharply, adjusting the strap of my bag. Then I lowered myself into the darkness below. The passage spit me out into the Undercity's filth, the stale air wrapping around me like a wet shroud. I had bypassed the gates, the monitors. I was back. The cold, industrial tunnels echoed with distant activity—muffled voices, the occasional hiss of steam.

I pulled my coat tighter, moving quickly. No one stopped me. No one paid any attention. That was the first rule down here—don't get involved. Lucian's hideout was nestled deep in a maze of forgotten corridors. The closer I got, the more my instincts sharpened. I wasn't being followed, but that didn't mean I wasn't being watched. The front door was unlocked, but that didn't mean I was welcome.

I stepped inside, shutting it behind me. Lucian was seated behind a low-lit desk, sifting through inventory logs. He barely glanced up, but the tension in the room thickened.

"Well. I see you made it back," he said, voice cool.

I unzipped my bag, pulling out the encryption devices. "And I brought you some goodies."

That got his attention. He sat back, reaching forward to take them from my hands. "What have we got here?"

I avoided his outreached hands, instead set the devices on the table between us. "A little conversation starter."

Lucien turn the unit in his hand.

"In case," I added "you know anyone who'd like a little privacy."

His gaze flicked between the hardware and

me, skepticism flickering across his face. "And your revenge?"

I exhaled, feigning frustration. "Didn't get to the bastard. Not yet." I lied

Lucian's eyes narrowed slightly.

I pushed forward before he could press the issue. "He's too well guarded. I ran out time setting the trap. These are just a little token of my appreciation."

Lucian picked up one of the devices, turning it in his hands. Then, slowly, he nodded. "That's very noble of you."

"I need to get back up there".

Lucian wasn't stupid. He didn't trust easily, and I had just done something incredibly difficult far too easily. He set the device down and nodded to one of his men. "Get these checked."

The man grabbed the devices and disappeared into a back room. Silence stretched between us as Lucian studied me.

"If they're clean, that'll be good news for you," he finally said.

The unspoken threat lingered between us.

I nodded once, leaning back in my chair. "I'm aware."

Minutes passed. I stayed still, steady. Then, finally, the runner returned.

"They're good," he confirmed. "Scrubbed twice over. No tracking signals, no trace."

Lucian's expression didn't change.

Satisfied, he stood, pushing up with his fingertips on the desk. "I'll let you know what my buyers have to say."

That was my cue to leave.

Rezik hadn't seen me return. However the moment I stepped back into his territory, his men closed in. Rough hands grabbed my arms, shoving me into the nearest wall.

Then came Rezik himself—angry, pacing. "Where the hell have you been? Where's the stuff?"

I shook him off, adjusting my coat. "Lucian has them."

Rezik's jaw tensed. "And why the hell wouldn't you come to me first?"

I shrugged. "I did what I said I'd do."

"That wasn't the deal."

"Wasn't it?" I tilted my head. "I don't remember agreeing to anything about that. Besides, I thought you and Lucien were ... a team." I emphasized the word team.

Rezik's eye twitched. His fingers flexed at his sides. "You don't decide things down here. You don't make deals without me."

I put my arms to my side, leaning my chest towards him, defiant. "I fulfilled the deal I made. What happens between you and your buh-" I caught myself on the letter 'B' of boyfriend and changed it "-business partner, is between you and him."

His nostrils flared. He took a step closer. I didn't move. His men watched, waiting for him to make a call. I held his gaze. Unflinching. Calm. This was his breaking point. Lucian had the power now. Rezik had nothing. And he knew it. Finally, he turned to his men.

"Wait here" he told them. "I need to pay Lucian a visit."

Then, to me— "You better hope I get what I'm owed."

I watched him go. I almost wanted to be a fly on the wall for this little lover's spat.

But Rezik was in a rare mood when he returned—dripping in luxury that had no business existing in the Undercity. A real leather coat, slick and pristine, hung off his shoulders. A gold pinky ring, glinting under the dim market lights. He handed each of us a fresh cigar, thick and fragrant, before pulling a bottle of scotch from inside his jacket and setting on the table.

"On me, boys" he said. Then he looked at me "Actually - on her!"

"You should be proud, Marla," he grinned, spreading his arms, taking up too much space. "Your little mission just put us on the map."

The others hooted and clapped him on the back.

"And this is just the beginning," he said. Then added "Lucien wants to see you."

I was startled and pleased. Pleased that I had managed to gain their confidence. Startled because I now had to take it to the next level. I needed to get to whoever bought those things.

The next day I went to see him.

Lucien didn't offer a greeting when I arrived. He was pacing. Always a bad sign.

"Your first shipment went through," he said without preamble.

"I figured, given Rezik's new taste in fashion."

Lucien shot me a look. "You know what that means, don't you? It worked. Your devices were real, and now I have a very interested buyer."

"Who?"

"Does it matter?"

My jaw clenched. I hated the way he danced around details. "Depends on what they want."

Lucien stopped pacing and turned to me. "Obviously, They want more."

"More encryption devices?"

"No, something bigger, Something much more valuable." He let me adsorb the significance of that. "Quantum-Key Distribution Nodes."

I stared at him, unbelieving. "You're kidding."

"Do I look like I'm joking?"

A few months ago, I had led a detail of enforcers working on a secretive cybersecurity update to the ISB building. What Lucian was asking for was enabling ultra-secure communication leveraging the properties of quantum mechanics. QKD nodes generate quantum bits (qubits), using a single photon of light in different quantum states. These qubits are transmitted to another node over a quantum channel, like fiber optics or free-space optics. This enables the transmission of data through free space using single-photon emitters.

QKD Nodes are high level government-security assets, the kind that governments in the past had used to dig out terrorist organizations - they are able to bridge secure data silos, information held in computers that are not directly connected to the network. Most people didn't even know such things existed. If they wanted this level, then I was definitely dealing with some high-level folks, and since it was in the Undercity, there was only one group that would need such devices. The rebels.

For the first time since I had been embedded here, my adrenaline surged, my heart raced, and I wondered if I could keep my composure. Getting a hold of myself, I pressed him for details.

"Your buyers must be pretty big players to need such insurgent level goods." I put emphasis on the word 'insurgent'.

Lucien bristled. "In my line of work, I learned not to ask those type of questions a long time ago. I suggest you learn the same."

I took a slow breath.

"You realize what you're asking for, right? That's not just contraband. That's next to impossible."

Lucien didn't blink. "You seem to manage the impossible."

"And they can afford such luxuries?"

"I assure you they will make this worth our while."

I narrowed my eyes. "Our? as in you and Rezik. Or as in we?" I took a step towards him, looking him straight in the eye. "What's in it for me? A wise man once told me its a pretty big favor to do something for people they hardly even know. And I'm not interested in scotch and cigars either. This time I want a cut."

Lucien thought a moment before he offered. "We're prepared to give you 25 percent."

I laughed. "You don't need me; you need a

therapist. You are not making me very motivated to help.

A slow silence settled between us.

"Half," I said.

Lucien arched a brow. "Shit..!"

"If you want me to do the impossible, I expect to get paid."

Lucien's fingers drummed the table for a minute, he was considering.

"Done." he said finally.

Within hours, I was above ground again, back inside ISB headquarters.

Like last time, I was met by two guards, but unlike last time I wasn't taken directly to the war room. This time, they led me down a side corridor and stopped at a decontamination chamber. I looked at the guard with a look of question on my face. Sliding the door open, he pointed to the pile of fresh clothes on the bench and towels and soap laid neatly beside them.

"The director gave strict orders."

I chuckled remembering how he had held his nose the last time I saw him. And I have to admit, a hot shower never felt better in my life!

After my shower, the guards standing outside the door snapped to attention when the door opened. They then led me to the war room where Locke and his team were waiting.

"Captain Rayne," Locke said, motioning for me to sit.

I took my place across from him, hands folded, posture straight. I didn't need them thinking the

Undercity had dulled my edges.

Locke leaned forward, lowering his glasses halfway down his nose. "You've been busy."

"I told you I would be."

"Fill me in."

"They took the bait," I said. "They want more."

Locke arched a brow. "Define 'more'."

I let the weight of it settle before I spoke. "Quantum-Key Distribution Nodes."

A silence stretched across the room, thick and loaded.

Lin's eyes narrowed. "Son of a b..."

Juric let out a low whistle, shaking his head. "They're not playing around anymore."

Locked leaned back slightly, his rising as he drew in a breath. "Interesting choice. What did they say they're going to do with them?"

I looked at him "They didn't say."

Lin glanced at him. "Maybe they don't even know yet. Could be they're stockpiling for later use."

Locke shook his head. "No. They have a target. My team has been decrypting the last few data leaks. The rebels have been mining the 'Final Process' files—searching for deleted citizens. They're digging up old data, trying to piece together the past. My guess? They want to go deeper. They need access to more of the purged files—ones that could be..." he paused, choosing his words carefully, "embarrassing to the Board."

I nodded. "That track. They were cagey about what exactly they needed it for, but they made it clear that I'm their best shot at getting it."

Locke considered that, then turned to Juric. "If we supply the nodes, how do we control them?"

Juric was already ahead of him. "We set them up with bio-metric encryption."

I frowned. "Meaning?"

Juric pointed at me. "Meaning you are the bio-metric key, Rayne."

I stared at him. "Come again?"

"The QKDNs won't activate without a registered bio-metric signature—yours."

Locke's gaze flicked back to me. "They'll have no choice but to bring you inside, Captain. It forces them to trust you. To reveal themselves."

I sat back, considering it.

It was a bold play. Risky as hell, but effective. The rebels had been dodging us for years—faceless, nameless, slipping through the cracks like smoke. But if they wanted this bad enough... they'd have to let me in.

I tapped my fingers against the table. "Alright. Let's say it works. Let's say I get in. Then what?"

Locke's smile didn't reach his eyes. "Then we shut them down."

"How?" I pressed. "You still can't extract me. And I might be good, but I can't take out an entire network by myself."

Juric sighed, rubbing his temples. "We're working on that."

I was about give Juric an idea about what I thought about that when suddenly the urgent chime of an incoming alert echoed through the room. It wasn't the usual notification—the kind one might ignore in favor of more pressing matters. This one was different.

It was a Priority-One System Alert.

My eyes flicked to the monitor behind Locke's chair, but the screen was locked from our view. Whatever it was, it wasn't for just anyone. It was for his eyes only.

Locke's demeanor shifted instantly. His jaw tensed as he leaned forward, tapping the screen to expand the alert. A deep red band reflected in his reading glasses told us this was the highest level of internal security clearance.

Juric raised an eyebrow.

Locke didn't move. His eyes scanned the data, fingers moving as he navigated through whatever the Algorithm had flagged. His expression didn't change—not at first—but something in the set of his shoulders told me this was serious.

No one spoke.

Juric and I exchanged glances.

A minute passed. Then two.

And then—very slowly—Locke lowered his head and pinched the bridge of his nose, his other hand waved over the screen closing the window. He remained motionless, which made it clear that this was something big, convoluted. Unexpected. None of us moved. None of us spoke. We just waited. And when Locke finally looked up, his expression unreadable, I felt the first trace of something I haven't felt in a long time. Fear.

Locke removed his reading glasses and carefully set them on the table in front of him. His eyes passing to each of us. No sign of emotion. His voice was calm, he'd obviously seen many things come through the system in the past. But there was something that had obviously shaken him, Something new even to him.

"Well." He sighed. "At least we know who we're dealing with now." He rubbed his face with his hand, pinching his eyes, then his nose and mouth before letting it grip his chin for a moment.

Lin straightened. Juric leaned in. I clenched my jaw.

His hand fell from his face.

"The data leaks. The ones we couldn't decrypt before? They aren't stealing information. They are trying to hide it. These so-called Rebels are targeting the core integrity of the Algorithm itself—burying logs of internal manipulation, manual overrides, protocol rewrites. All done quietly. All done carefully."

Lin's eyes narrowed. "What kind of overrides?"

Locke tapped his fingers against the desk, watching the screen. "Subtle ones. Just small enough to go unnoticed. Adjusting SES scores here and there, altering records, shifting parameters of behavioral compliance ratings. Almost as if they were testing thresholds, seeing what they could get away with."

Juric's hands clenched. "They're staging a coup."

Locke finally looked up at him, sharp and assessing. "May be."

Juric exhaled sharply. "If they're attempting to take control of the system..."

Locke held up a hand, cutting him off.

"They may already have it. They've been good at keeping the system from seeing them. Pretty well hidden." He nodded suggesting he was almost… almost, impressed. "But unlike the Algorithm, they are fallible."

All of us hung on to those words, not wanting to interrupt.

"Luckily for us, they got sloppy," Locke continued. "The Algorithm just identified the pattern. And it has identified the players."

The room remained dead silent.

Lin was the first to break it. "Who?"

Locke exhaled, finally leaning back in his chair. His voice was quieter.

"It seems our rebels… are the Oligarchs themselves."

The words hit like a sledgehammer.

For a long moment, no one spoke.

Lin blinked. "How is that … even possible?"

Juric let out something between a scoff and a hollow laugh. "I knew it. They've been playing the system this entire time."

Locke didn't answer, ignoring the obvious lack of confidence in the Board.

We all knew what this meant. This wasn't some underground resistance. This wasn't a few rogue citizens hacking from the shadows, trying to bring down the state. This was the men who ran New Columbia. And suddenly, everything we thought we knew? Had now just changed.

"Sir?" I asked, struggling for the right words. "That means … my mission … is now to go after our own Board?" The question felt like it barely belonged in my mouth. "How do we proceed?"

Locke's gaze was distant, his fingers steepled as he absorbed the weight of what we had just uncovered. He had obviously been grappling with the same conundrum.

"We do what we've always done," he said at last, his voice even, measured.

"We protect Callus. We protect the Algorithm. And we resolve this little problem before the people of New Columbia ever find out."

His words rang in my ears. I had a mission to finish.

Locke leaned back, looking hard at me.

"Captain Rayne. You think you can get in?"

I nodded. "Yes, sir."

"Then get back in," he ordered. "Offer them what they want."

I hesitated. "Sir, with all due respect—how does this help us?"

Locke exhaled sharply through his nose.

"Because they need those files, Rayne. The moment they plug those Quantum Keys into the system, we'll have a backdoor into the same data. We'll recover what they're after—the erased identities. The proof of who they are. And then, we wipe them out before they ever reclaim their power."

It clicked into place. This was preemptive deletion. A kill switch.

"Understood," I said, my voice steady.

Locke nodded once. "Get it done."

Chapter 20

THE TRAP IS SET

Adam stood motionless as lines of code scrolled across the monitors, feeding into the system in calculated bursts. My fingers clenched into a fist as I watched. This was it. The moment we'd been working toward.

The team had spent hours embedding the patterns—tiny inconsistencies, misalignment, and invisible breadcrumbs that The Watchers, the Algorithm's compliance monitors, were designed to detect. We weren't breaking in. We weren't forcing our way through firewalls. We were letting the system discover us—feeding it reports it expected, trusted. Leaving certain details, originally hidden, exposed in a way that would make it think it had uncovered the discrepancies itself. And once it did, it wouldn't be able to ignore them.

I remembered the night I'd first stumbled onto the hidden logs, buried so deep in the system's command history that they would never have been detected. Manual overrides. Selective visibility protocols. Behavioral nudging scripts. The Board hadn't just been using The Algorithm to govern—they'd been rewriting its rules in real-time, bending it to serve their own interests while the rest of the city believed in its infallibility. And Callus had no idea.

The man who built his empire on order, control, perfection—the one who had preached for years that The Algorithm was pure, unerring, untouched by human greed—had been played like a fool. The Oligarchs had rewritten the rules in their favor, deciding which of us would rise, who fell, and who disappeared into the abyss of the Undercity. It wasn't governance. It was a rigged game. And as long as they stayed in power, no one could ever win but them. That night, when I first uncovered the truth, I had thought I was alone. I thought that maybe I was the only one who had seen the cracks in the system. But now, sitting in the heart of the Ghost Network's headquarters, I watched as Adam and his team used those very same cracks to bring it all crashing down on them.

A sharp beep from the console snapped me back to the present. Adam and I leaned over Clarence's shoulder and watched his monitors. I felt Adam tense.

"It's working," Clarence said excitedly. "The system just flagged an irregularity."

Moments later another ... then another.

I smiled. We caught their attention.

Now it was just a matter of time before flags became patterns. But we still had the problem of getting into the News data silos to access the "approved" stories so I could take care of step two in our plan. To give the system encouragement by making it think the irregularities had been approved for public consumption. Across from me, Adam sat hunched over a stack of hastily scrawled notes, rubbing his temple as if trying to push back a headache. His fingers tapped against the edge of the table, sharp and impatient.

As if on cue, Lee burst in, delivering the solution.

"Good news. Bad news. Boss" On the news story front."

Adam leaned forward. "Run that by me again?"

Lee—dressed in their usual over-sized coat, who had just come in from the depth of the Undercity— seemed to enjoy her role as the eyes and ears of what was happening 'down in'.

"Quantum Key Distribution Nodes are in play," they said. "Lucien's mole pulled through. He says to tell you he's ready to deliver them."

Adam exhaled in relief. "I take it that's the good news."

"Well," Lee continued, dragging the word out, "they're bio-metrically locked. Meaning the carrier has to be physically present to install them. He wants to know if the deal is still on."

Silence.

Adam's head dropped into his hands. "Of course," he muttered. "Of course, that's how they'd be configured. I should've considered that."

"Not the kind of thing you forget, boss," Clarence piped up from the other side of the room, still glued to his monitor. "That's high-security hardware. My hunch is they are rigged to self-destruct without the key."

Adam didn't pay him any attention. I could see he

was considering our options to decide the next move.

I frowned. "Bio-metric key?"

Lee spoke before Adam could open his mouth. "The keys must be verified biologically by someone who has been authorized to engage them. And before you suggest we kill them and cut off their finger to press the buttons ... I thought of that ... the key only activates from a living organism, so you'd have to be pretty quick. Or, they have to come in... activate the key and then we kill them right after ..."

My gut tightened and Adam laughed.

"Lee, you've been watching movies again. We aren't going to kill anyone. Not unless we have to."

I almost felt relieved but couldn't be sure if he was joking or not. He had spent months—years—making sure no one unaccounted for got this deep into our network. Now we were about to roll out the welcome mat for some newbie smuggler?

Adam pinched the bridge of his nose, clenching his jaw, serious again. "We don't have a choice."

I opened my mouth to say something, but he cut me off.

"We're out of time. The Algorithm has already started flagging the activity. Right now, it's noticing patterns. Give it another day—maybe two—and it's going to start correcting them. Without back-up news releases to make it think the reports are not classified, everything we'd worked for—the reports, the leaks, the slow unraveling of the Oligarchs' control over the system—it would all be buried. Discredited. Erased.

I knew Adam was right. We had one shot at this.

If we didn't move now, we'd lose our window.

"Who is this carrier?" I asked, finally.

Lee shrugged. "Lucien calls her 'Marla Sedgewick.' Supposedly an ex-financial officer, offloaded for catching a high-ranking exec with his hand in the SES credit jar."

"Sounds convenient," I muttered.

"Yeah, well, Lucien says she's been useful," Lee replied. "And the guy isn't exactly generous with his trust."

Adam exhaled rubbing the back of his neck. "She has the keys. We need them." He stood up, rolling his shoulders like he was bracing for impact.

"Lee, send for her. Let's see where this goes."

Twenty minutes later the room had shifted. A quiet tension settled over us as we waited for our guest to arrive. Clarence had powered down his monitors, making sure no identifiable information was left in the open. Adam's eyes were scanning the room for anything that could tip off a spy. Across the room, Lee had gone quiet, which was rare. I stood with my hands on my hips, watching the door.

The entrance slid open. And she stepped in.

She moved with the confidence of someone who knew how to handle themselves—shoulders squared, chin lifted just slightly, dark eyes scanning the room in an instant. She was smaller than I expected. Lean. Controlled. But there was something else. Something off. I tried to place it.

Adam gave a tight nod. "You must be Marla."

The woman's gaze snapped to him. "I am," she

said smoothly. Her voice was steady. Even. Too even. Lucien was right. She was well trained.

"And you are?" She responded.

"I am" he agreed, obviously refusing to answer.

She seemed to accept it. I watched as Adam gestured for her to sit. She didn't move right away. Just took us all in, one by one. Calculating. Assessing. Like a lone wolf sizing up the pack. I immediately disliked her. Then her eyes landed on me. For a fraction of a second, something flickered in her expression. Recognition. Then, gone. Something in the way she looked at me told me we had just gotten off to a bad start.

Adam leaned back, his eyes—calculating, sharp—never leaving the woman in front of him. Marla Sedgewick. Or at least, that's who she claimed to be. She looked the part. I'd give her that. If I hadn't already spent enough time in the Undercity to recognize a survivor when I saw one, I might have believed her. But something was off. She was someone whom the Undercity hadn't yet defeated. Adam felt it too. His voice was casual, almost lazy, but I could see the way his fingers tapped against his bicep. Measuring her.

"You'll understand if we need to be sure about you," he said.

Marla—Evelyn—tilted her head, giving him a tired look. "Of course. I'd be worried if you didn't."

"Let's talk about the keys, then," Adam said. "Quantum Key Distribution nodes aren't exactly the kind of thing you pick up in a back alley. How did a finance clerk like you get access to something most people don't even know exists?"

A flicker of something passed over her face. Surprise? No—something practiced. She had expected this question.

"My old boss," she said, voice tightening. "He's why I'm down here. The bastard had me offloaded me to save himself." Her fists clenched, her breathing sharp. It looked real. It felt real. The kind of raw, bitter anger that is hard to fake.

Adam let her go on.

"He had connections. One of his old high school buddies—who had become a National Security engineer—they grew up together, still played golf. My boss used to help him out now and then."

"Help him out how?" Adam asked, watching her carefully.

She met his eyes. "Selling SES points. Kept him from losing security clearance on several occasions. And as you know, keeping security clearance when you don't deserve it is kind of a no-no in the upper tiers"

I glanced at Lee. Their jaws tightened. That wasn't just minor corruption. It could be construed as treason by New Columbia's own standards.

Marla didn't flinch. "I knew about it. And suddenly I found myself down here. Then I met Lucien and had a way up to the surface. I could finally extract my revenge. But Lucien pimped me out to you guys, so... I found the guy, appeared to him like a demon from the afterlife. I told him I needed the keys, or I'd make sure he joined me down here in hell."

Adam raised an eyebrow. "How do we know he won't come after us. Can you assure us that he isn't setting us up?"

Her eyes narrowed as she looked at the members in this room. "Because I told him I was working with an Oligarch," she said smoothly. "Someone important. Someone who needed to recover some... embarrassing ... let's say personal files locked in an inaccessible silo."

That got Adam's attention. I caught the faint twitch of his fingers. This was a dangerous game we were all playing.

"He believed you?" Adam asked.

Marla shrugged. "People believe things if they stand to gain from it. I told him there would be plenty of money in it for him once the job was done."

Adam exchanged a glance with Lee. I could tell that they were assessing her story and coming to the same conclusion. It wasn't airtight. No. A little messy, full of desperation, but just enough risk and self-serving to make sense. It seemed believable.

Until she made her mistake.

"So, in order to cut him in, the price is a little higher than we discussed," Marla added smoothly, flicking an invisible speck of dust from her sleeve. "But I figure with your connections to the Board, that won't be a problem, don't you agree?"

Chapter 21

ENEMY OF MY ENEMY

Adam remained calm after the obvious highball efforts by Marla to renegotiate the terms—almost too calm. As soon as she mentioned a price, he casually glanced down at the small screen on his wrist and pressed a button. He looked up at Marla, his face was neutral.

"I'm sure we can work something out," he said smoothly.

But there was something in the way he had said it, as if the price didn't matter. He suddenly became softer, less edgy. Instead of suspicion that he had shown before, he just sounded polite. As if he'd made up his mind.

Marla watched him carefully as well as trying to tell if she had passed whatever test Adam had been giving her. I saw her fingers twitch, adjusting the sleeve of her coat, then catching herself and forcing herself into stillness. She was good at controlling her reactions.

Adam, however, remained unconcerned.

"We're going to need some time to prepare for the transfer," he continued, glancing back at his wrist. "Give us…" he pressed a button, reading something that only he could see. "... give us ten hours."

He turned to Lee, pointing to his watch.

"Lee, I just got a notice that we have an unexpected visitor. Code Three. Can you see to it they move along?"

Lee, who had been leaning against the far wall, barely looked at Adam before pushing off and heading straight for the exit. No hesitation. No questions.

Code Three. I didn't know the exact meaning, but I knew enough. A threat had just been identified.

Marla didn't react at first, but I saw the way her weight shifted, her stance adjusting ever so slightly. She was listening. Calculating. I forced my expression into something neutral. Adam turned back to her with a practiced smile and stepped forward, gently taking her arm.

"Marla, It was delightful meeting you. We're good on this end. Why don't you go back to your quarters and get some rest?"

His voice was light, easy. A friendly, courteous suggestion.

"We'll be ready for you at 1800 hours, and we'll arrange for your payment once the keys are activated."

For a moment, Marla didn't move. I could almost see her mind working, processing everything at once. Was she suspicious? Did she think she'd been made?

"What are you offering to guarantee my safety once the keys are activated. After all, my services might be deemed -" she hesitated for effect "- a liability once they've been activated."

Adam kept his hands on her arm. "Ah! Yes. No

honor among thieves, is there? I get that. It's all part of the negotiation process. You knew that coming in. But I give you my word. I need the keys, and once I have them, I won't need to worry be in hiding anymore, so there's no reason not to keep my end of the bargain. You're asking to be paid for services rendered and I am civilized enough to grant you that."

After a beat, she gave a tight nod. "Fine."

She turned on her heel and left. I didn't exhale until the door slid shut behind her. Silence stretched between me and Adam for a long moment before he finally turned to me.

I frowned. "What just happened?"

He nodded, tapping the screen on his wrist again. "Code Three means she's been marked as a potential enemy of the network." He glanced at the exit. "I sent Lee to keep an eye on her. Without tipping Marla off. Marla is not our friend."

A slow chill crept down my spine.

"Wait," I said, lowering my voice. "What gave her away?"

Adam folded his arms. "She thinks we're in with the Oligarchs."

"Yeah, I caught that," I said. "But why would that matter?"

Adam was already steps ahead. I could see the gears turning in his head.

"The only way she'd assume that is if she was aware of our transmissions," he said.

I opened my mouth—then closed it.

That... that might be a problem.

Adam turned to Clarence, who was already pulling up the system interface on the nearest terminal. "Run a high-resolution deep scan on our outgoing messages," Adam instructed. "Not just our payload. I want to see the waveforms themselves."

"Payload?" I asked

"The actual content of the encrypted transmissions," Adam said barely noticing me.

"What are we looking for?" I continued.

"I don't know yet. Anything out of the ordinary; timing inconsistencies, frequency modulations, and data packet behaviors."

Clarence's fingers flew over the keyboard. Lines of code streamed across the screen in rapid succession.

I leaned over his shoulder as the analysis began compiling. For a long moment, there was nothing. Then the wave forms came up. Clarence took a closer look, then leaned back. Damn!" he muttered,

"How the hell did I miss that?"

"I don't see it," Adam said, "what do you see?"

Clarence pointed to a section of the waveform. Barely perceptible, buried within the layers of signal interference the encryption created, was a tiny portion of the wave that was just out of sync. a very slight echo effect—a near-identical data packet being sent milliseconds after the original. It's subtle, something that hadn't shown up in a standard scan. Sensing that I was lost, Adam turned to me and explained.

"The encryption devices should be sending only one stream of data, but something is piggybacking on the outgoing signal. That means ..." he looked at Clarence, then to me. "Someone—besides the Watchers—was getting our feed."

My stomach dropped.

"Whoever supplied Marla with the encryption devices set up the network to expose itself," Clarence pointed out.

Adam exhaled slowly; his hand reached across himself to rub his bicep. I could feel the weight of what this meant pressing down on all of us.

I swallowed. "So… what now?"

Adam grinned. A real, genuine grin. I blinked.

"Adam?"

Shaking his head, he looked jubilant "Iris, we just got the perfect cover."

I stared.

He gestured toward the screen. "If the ISB thinks the Board is behind the resistance and have sent Marla to expose the Board…"

I exhaled, pressing my fingers to my temples trying to keep up.

Now Clarence had caught on. Smiling, he filled me in.

"We share a common goal. She's going to help us expose the Board for what it is. Like they say, the enemy of my enemy…"

Chapter 22

A WORLD OUTSIDE THE CITY

I watched the progress bar crawl forward on the monitor, each percentage point bringing us closer to detonating the truth. My fingers hovered near the keyboard, prepared to counteract any system rollback, but so far—nothing. The Algorithm wasn't rejecting the upload. It wasn't flagging it, altering it, or dissolving it into propaganda. It was accepting it.

I attempted to calm my breathing, forcing my hands to steady. This was it. This was real. Adam and Clarence had worked through the night, planting the fractures in the system's logic, slowly feeding it just enough inconsistency for it to recognize something was wrong. Now, we weren't just slipping past the Algorithm's defenses—we were making it see the truth. The screen flickered, and then the headlines appeared, generated by the very system meant to suppress them.

BREAKING NEWS:
LEADER CALLUS IDENTIFIES INTERNAL
THREAT WITHIN THE BOARD
MERITOCRACY UNDER ATTACK FROM WITHIN

I stared at the text, unable to breathe. We'd done it! This wasn't being flagged as anti-Columbia. This was an official announcement—the Algorithm itself had corroberated the story. We had hijacked reality.

Adam let out a low whistle, arms crossed. "And just like that… it begins."

I turned to look at Marla. She hadn't moved since the moment the stories went live. She was standing near the terminal, her hands flat on the desk, breathing just a little too carefully—too measured, too controlled. The air around her had shifted, the way it does just before a thunderstorm cracks the sky open. My heart pounded, but I kept my expression neutral. I tilted my head slightly, studying her the way she had studied me so many times before. Waiting. Calculating. Then I spoke.

"Just a matter of time, huh, Evelyn?"

I watched her entire body go rigid. Slowly, she turned to face me, her expression a perfect mask of indifference—but I could see the muscle in her jaw tighten, the tension around her mouth. I had her.

"I knew you'd track me down eventually," I continued, my voice soft, almost amused. "I'm Iris, pleased to meet you. You've been looking for me. I believe you wanted to capture me pretty badly, didn't you?

I could see her mind racing, piecing together what had just happened. She wasn't stupid. She was one of the most dangerous enforcers in New Columbia, trained to read a room in a second, to anticipate threats before they became threats. But this—this she hadn't expected. A bead of sweat traced down the side of her neck. Not much, but enough.

I stepped closer.

"Now there seems to be a question of who caught who."

Evelyn blinked, her expression not betraying anything—but she didn't speak. That silence told me everything. She was thinking. Thinking too much. And Evelyn Rayne only overthought when she was losing control. I let that realization settle in before I delivered the final blow.

"What's wrong, Captain?" I asked, voice smooth. "You look like you've just seen a Ghost."

For the first time since I had met her, Evelyn Rayne didn't know what to do next. And that terrified her. She stood rigid, her whole body locked in place like she'd just been shot through the spine. Her face was unreadable, but I could see it happening—the fracture forming behind her eyes.

She was unraveling. Slowly. Quietly. And the worst part? I don't think she even realized it yet.

"You thought you were going to stop the resistance?" Adam's voice was calm, but there was a sharp edge beneath it. A quiet kind of triumph. He didn't smirk this time. He didn't gloat. He just let the words settle. "I hate to tell you, but you just brought down the Board."

Evelyn flinched. It was small, barely noticeable, but it was there. "No, not ... I wanted to stop the lies. You've been misleading people. Feeding them lies."

The way she said it, I could tell she wanted it to

be true.

Adam tilted his head. "Are we?"

He gestured toward the monitors, where the headlines were still flashing, rippling through the system unchecked. No counter-narratives. No corrections. No automated suppression. The Algorithm wasn't fighting the information. It was processing it. Accepting it. Like it had been waiting for it.

"Your perfect Algorithm here seems to agree. These aren't lies."

I saw the moment Evelyn realized it too. Her fingers twitched at her sides, holding her breath for the smallest second before she smothered it beneath her enforcer steel.

"No..." she gasped, barely loud enough to hear.

Adam took a step forward. Not aggressive. Just certain.

"The Algorithm was being manipulated by the board. ," he said. "It always has been."

She shook her head, her whole body rejecting it. Refusing to believe what her eyes were telling her...

"You don't ..." she started, then halted. "I don't understand ...the system ... " her voice trailed off, watching the news headlines "...is infallible."

Adam exhaled sharply. Not quite a laugh. Not quite anything.

"Evelyn," he said, voice lower now. "You've spent your whole life believing in it. Trusting it. Because that's what they, Callus and the Oligarchs, needed you to do." He tilted his head. "But the Algorithm isn't some divine, untouchable intelligence. It's a machine."

"A perfect machine," Evelyn snapped.

"A machine built to serve the Board and Callus, not you, not us," Adam countered.

The second fracture in her belief, her faith, showed a crack. Evelyn sucked in a sharp breath, but she didn't step back. Didn't retreat. She was fighting it. Fighting herself. Fighting the part of her brain that was starting to see the pattern—the discrepancies she'd never allowed before.

"It's sucking me in. I need to resist the pull of the Undercity," she chanted to herself, her voice cracking. "I've trained for this—"

"Evelyn, wake up" Adam shouted. "We are not the ones luring you into deception, they are! It's right in front of you. The Oligarchs control the Algorithm to keep people like you doing their bidding! You are a tool in their machinery. The feelings you are now feeling are not a lie, they are reality telling you to wake up!"

I watched Evelyn's hands clench into fists at her sides. She was losing ground, and she knew it. The thing about belief is that it doesn't just disappear all at once. It cracks, it falters, but it doesn't shatter. Not yet. She was trying to hold onto the pieces, but the proof was ripping them away.

And then Clarence spoke.

"Uh…" He hesitated. Confused. Almost nervous. "Guys… I think you should see this."

I turned toward him. So did Adam. Evelyn didn't move. Clarence was hunched over his console, fingers moving frantically across the keyboard, his face bathed in the pale glow of the screen. His brows knitted together as he worked, his expression shifting from focused to uneasy.

"I was running a deep scan through the purged archives," he said, still typing. "Checking for anything the system might use to restore us—to 'unerase' the Ghosts." He paused, his fingers hovering for a second before resuming at double speed. "I wasn't even looking for this, but..." He trailed off, shaking his head. "Holy shit."

"Clarence," Adam's voice was sharp now. "What did you find?"

Clarence looked up. He looked shaken.

"External Media."

He gestured at the screen, then looked at Adam and I. "A folder labeled 'External Media.' It's full of rejected news segments." He hesitated, shaking his head. "These are reports. News broadcasts, government correspondences, economic analyses... from outside New Columbia."

Silence settled over the room like a tightening vise.

"Clarence, outside New Columbia is devastated. Hardly worth reporting on," Adam said carefully, though his voice was tight. "At least, not in any way that still matters. The world ended. We're it."

"I understand" Clarence agreed quickly. His eyes flicked back to the screen, scanning the impossible reality in front of him. "But if that's true, explain this—" He tapped a key, pulling up the first file. The screen flickered. A news broadcast. A real one. A polished anchor sat behind a sleek news desk, a bright skyline sprawling in the background—not New Columbia. Lush. Clean. Thriving. A ticker across the bottom of the screen showed the date of publication - the date was this week. Adam stiffened, jaw tightening. "Could be a hack - a deep fake." His voice was flat, but there was a thread of something behind it. "Maybe someone else has been here before us—we could have another group to compete with—"

"I kind of doubt it," Clarence interrupted, shaking his head. "I did some checking on the metadata. These aren't planted files. There's no external tampering, no signs of forced insertion. These records were monitored, logged, processed, and stored just like every other media file in the system." He hesitated, fingers drumming anxiously on the desk. "But here's the kicker—" He tapped another key, bringing up a set of timestamps. "The Algorithm didn't reject these reports as fake news. It didn't flag them for manipulation or external interference..."

The room dropped into dead silence.

"It just decided they weren't fit for publication and deleted them."

Everyone in the room, all of us, stood with mouths gaping. It just wasn't possible. Because the outside world didn't exist. Couldn't exist. The world outside New Columbia had collapsed. That was history. That was a fact. This was like saying the earth is flat. A ridiculous notion.

Chapter 23

LOCKE'S FINAL SOLUTION

The Internal Security Bureau never slept.

Deep within the ISB headquarters, Director Marius Locke stood before a wall of surveillance monitors, his hands clasped tightly behind his back. His jaw tightened as lines of cascading data scrolled across the screens—red warning glyphs flashing against the dim blue glow of the command center.

A system-wide alert had just been triggered. One of the analysts nearby swore under his breath.

"Sir… "

Locke's gaze snapped to the terminal as the feed loaded. The news ticker was already running across every official channel:

BREAKING NEWS
SYSTEM TAMPERING DETECTED
LEADER UNCOVERS INTERNAL SABOTAGE
OLIGARCHS INVESTIGATED FOR
MANIPULATING ALGORYTHM—JUSTICE WILL
BE SERVED

Locke's stomach twisted. This wasn't a breach. This wasn't an attack from foreign enemies. This was the Algorithm itself reporting on an internal conspiracy. That wasn't supposed to happen.

"This is impossible," Juric muttered from his station, his hands flying over the interface as he ran diagnostics. "The Algorithm should have flagged these reports for review. There are protocols—we built the safeguards into the system."

Locke exhaled slowly, forcing himself to think. He had suspected for weeks that someone was leaking data from the Undercity, but now? The system had compiled the data itself—processed it, validated it, and broadcast it without authorization. This wasn't a hack. This was the machine turning against them. His gaze drifted to a secondary data stream—security alerts pinging across the network. The Algorithm had tagged the Oligarchs for investigation. Some were already being detained by their own security forces. Others had gone dark, their SES profiles locked in recursive loops, flagged for "compliance review."

The cracks were spreading too fast.

"Damn it." Locke turned sharply on his heel. "Get me Callus. Now."

Presidential Quarters, Executive District

The room smelled of stale alcohol and antiseptic. Orin Callus sat behind his massive black-marble desk, a tumbler of whiskey resting in his thick fingers, the amber liquid swirling lazily with each twitch of his wrist. The walls around him flickered with news feeds, a hundred shifting images of his own face, his own name, headlines painting him as the vigilant leader, the savior of New Columbia.

Callus leaned back, smiling. "You see that, Locke?" He gestured vaguely at the screens. "They love me."

Locke kept his expression neutral. "Sir, the Algorithm has flagged every Oligarch on the Board for investigation. It's exposed the internal tampering."

"Good." Callus took a slow sip, his eyes never leaving the screens. "The Board betrayed me. I always knew it. This proves it."

Locke's fingers curled into his palm. He doesn't understand.

"Sir, the Algorithm is out of control," Locke pressed. "It's moving without oversight. If we don't shut it down—"

Callus slammed his glass onto the desk, the sound sharp and sudden.

"Shut it down?" His eyes flashed dangerously. "The system is working. Look at this." He jabbed a thick finger at the ticker running across the largest screen.

THE LEADER UNCOVERS TRAITORS
LOYAL CITIZENS STAND WITH CALLUS

Callus spread his arms, his smile widening. "It's doing exactly what it's supposed to do."

Locke fought the urge to grind his teeth.

"You don't get it," Locke said carefully through clenched jaw. "We didn't tell it to do this. It made these connections on its own. It exposed the Oligarchs because their actions were inconsistent with its core logic."

"Then we let it finish the job," Callus said smoothly.

Locke inhaled sharply. "Sir, you are not in control of this narrative anymore."

Callus chuckled, shaking his head as if Locke were a naive child. "Of course I am. The people want order. They want me."

Locke hesitated.

This was not the man he had pledged his loyalty to. The Orin Callus of ten years ago had been sharp, calculating, ruthless, but rational. But this self-assured, self-obsessed egomaniac in front of him wasn't looking for solutions. He was basking in the chaos.

"Lock it down." Callus said, waving his hand dismissively. "Purge the Board. I'm declaring martial law."

"Sir, I strongly advise—"

Callus' expression darkened. "Did I ask for your advice, Locke?"

Locke froze. A slow, crawling realization settled over him. This wasn't just about the Algorithm glitching. Callus wanted this purge. He wanted the Oligarchs gone; the entire system restructured around him. This was more than a political maneuver. This was a cleansing. A purge. And Locke knew, in that moment, his own loyalty was now suddenly in question. The board were cowards, he knew that. And the thought of Algorithm let loose without boundaries was terrifying. In an instant Locke weighed his options and placed his bet with Callus.

"Of course, sir," Locke said stiffly. "I'll see to it personally."

Callus grinned. "That's why I keep you around, Locke."

ISB Headquarters – Crisis Command Center

Locke returned to the command floor, his mind racing. His operatives were already in motion—locking down SES profiles, scrubbing data streams, isolating key figures for detainment. The Board was eating itself alive, each Oligarch accusing the others, some already fleeing, trying to erase their own footprints.

Lin turned as he approached, her expression tight. "Sir. Orders?"

Locke exhaled slowly. For the first time in his career, he hesitated. Not because he didn't know what to do. But because he did.

He turned toward the central command console, eyes scanning the cascading security reports. Evelyn Rayne. Her name was still there. Still in the system. Still tied to the ISB. A liability.

His fingers hovered over the display before he turned sharply to Juric. "Callus has declared martial law. He's purging anyone with ties to the Oligarchs.

We need to distance ourselves from our operative."

Juric's brows furrowed slightly. "Sir?"

Locke didn't look away from the screen. "Rayne compromised herself. The rebels have her." His voice was cold, absolute. "If we act now, we control the narrative. If we hesitate, she becomes their weapon against us."

Lin's fingers tensed against the edge of the console. "You want to—"

"Erase her," Locke said flatly. "Purge her SES. Final Process. Effective immediately."

Juric hesitated. "Sir, if she's still alive, she—"

"She doesn't exist anymore." Locke's tone left no room for argument. He turned to Lin. "Push the announcement. We make it official before they do."

Lin swallowed, then nodded. A few keystrokes, a single command.

ASSET TERMINATED

Locke watched as the screen refreshed, her profile dissolving into nothing.

He turned back to his operatives. "Now," he said, his voice razor-sharp, "let's finish cleaning this mess up. Find a way to get our Enforcers into the Undercity."

Chapter 24

THE FINAL BETRAYAL

In the days that followed, New Columbia did not collapse as we expected. Not in flames, not in riots, not in the great rebellion we once imagined. The Board, the very Oligarchs which were now declared to be enemies of Callus, still held the controls on the Algorithm. They could not be touched, and although they no longer held official positions, they had not relinquished power. They simply vanished from public sight, looting everything on their way out, draining bank reserves, funneling wealth into shell corporations, and hiding their wealth in accounts that didn't technically exist.

The SES system was in shambles, entire sectors of the city crumbled under economic free fall. There was no money, no government stability, no way to support the common person. I suspected that the Oligarchs were too rich, too powerful, to be completely brought down. But I had gambled that if we could use them as a pawn. If we could show just how broken the system really was, we would see the people turn on Callus, to destroy him for creating such a weak and imperfect system. I had expected to see his head on a pike paraded through the streets. Or at least, for god's sake, a little public jeering.

But instead?

Callus still had them. The people. They were not fighting back. They didn't blame him. They rallied behind him, chanting in the streets, demanding that he restore order. Rebuild. He admitted the system was broken. Once again, he simply claimed that he alone could fix it. More efficient. More perfect. And once again, they believed him. I stood in front of the monitors, arms crossed, watching a broadcast loop of Callus addressing the city. Charismatic as ever.

"We will not be defeated. We will rebuild."

Adam exhaled sharply beside me. In our news releases we had portrayed him as having been betrayed.

"We convinced them that he was a victim. They think he's one of them."

I let those words sink in. I had just handed Callus more power. He was the perfect villain, the perfect charlatan, and somehow—somehow—they loved him more for it. My plan had backfired.

"How can they rebuild if the Oligarchs still run the Algorithm?" I asked Adam who had turned away, no longer watching the speech. He seemed genuinely disinterested in their games now.

"He'll bring them back, somehow." he sighed. "He knows he can't control without their blessings so all this will be for nothing. Just another show in a never-ending reality TV plot line. Things will go right back to the way they were."

"And ... what happens to us?

"And .. now we are the ones trapped."

Suddenly Lee burst into the room, their faces drenched in sweat, gasping for breath.

"Adam," they choked out, gripping the door frame. "The bookstore… enforcers… they are coming down the fire escape—"

Adam was at their side in an instant, steadying them. "Okay, okay, slow down. What's happening?"

Lee swallowed hard, their words coming fast and tight. "Enforcers. In the Undercity. They came in through the bookstore opening."

Adam's face darkened. "The bookstore?"

Evelyn straightened at the news, her face bore a look of relief and amusement. "I had the building scanned. We found your entrance. Hope you don't mind some visitors."

The smugness in her voice made my blood boil. Clarence was already at the monitors, fingers flying across the interface. The main screen flickered to life—a high-angle security feed from outside the bookstore where Adam had first introduced himself to me. The alley was crawling with movement. Dark figures in tactical gear.

"The system is designed to keep the offloaded down here" Adam pointed out. "Why aren't they affected?"

Clarence's fingers flew over the controls, switching to a secondary surveillance overlay. The screen flickered as he activated a passive electromagnetic scan, a technique used to detect disruptions in the natural EM field of an environment. The feed shifted, layering a ghostly wave of ionized interference patterns over the images outside The Second Chapter, the bookstore used to enter the Undercity. The enforcers appeared as dark silhouettes, but around their heads and upper bodies, a strange null zone formed—a break in the typical EM field distribution. Clarence narrowed his eyes.

"That's not standard counter-surveillance gear," he muttered. He adjusted the scan parameters, increasing the sensitivity. The voids around the enforcers began to pulse faintly, like heat signatures obscured by an invisible shroud.

"EMT shields," he murmured under his breath.

"What?" Adam demanded.

Clarence tapped a command, isolating the distortions into a spectral frequency. A ripple effect ran through the data. "They're using disruption fields," he said, spinning his chair toward Adam. "Low-frequency pulse modulation. It scrambles the cognitive imprint that the Algorithm uses to condition offloaded minds."

Adam swore.

"Translation?" I pressed.

"They're cloaked," Clarence said grimly. "The Algorithm can't map them. The Undercity's neurological conditioning doesn't touch them."

"They're coming to extract me," Evelyn chided. She couldn't help but smile.

I turned sharply toward her. "They're looking for us. And you—" I held her gaze, unflinching, "you are now one of us."

Evelyn scoffed. "I've almost fallen for the Undercity's mind-traps more than once, but this?" She pointed at the screen, shaking her head. "These are my people. They're coming to bring me back to my senses."

Clarence's voice cut through the tension. "I'm getting bio-metric scans."

Adam's head snapped toward him. "Say that again?"

Clarence's fingers moved furiously across the keyboard. "They're using old-school DNA detection devices." He looked up, face pale. "This is not good, Adam. We don't have blockers for DNA scans. They don't need visuals. They just need time. And if we stay here, they will find us."

A sly grin now grew into a full smile across Evelyn's face.

"Ghost-busters," she murmured.

Evelyn stood watching as the enforcers forced their way through the small fire escape and into the streets of the market. The signature of bio-metric scanners glowed on the screen as they swept through the Undercity. She thought they were here for her. That all she had to do was step forward and she'd be taken back, reinstated, restored to her perfect little world.

But I knew better. I had known for days. It was just after I had uploaded the Callus cover stories—manufacturing the illusion of his righteous crusade against the Oligarchs, feeding the system just enough truth to make the lie believable. After the stories had gone live, I'd stayed in the system, scrolling through the Algorithm's back end, watching how it adjusted, how it adapted. And that was when I had seen it. Now it was time to play my card.

I turned to Clarence.

"Pull up Evelyn Rayne's SES."

Evelyn snapped her head towards me. Clarence hesitated, glancing between me and Adam. Adam gave him a single nod.

A few keystrokes later, the screen flickered, and there it was.

ASSET TERMINATED

Evelyn went pale. Her mouth opened slightly, but no words came out. Her eyes darted from the screen to me, back to the screen, as if looking at it long enough would change the words staring her in the face.

"Wha…?" Her voice cracked. "No. That's… That's wrong."

I stepped forward, keeping my voice steady. "They terminated you, Evelyn." I watched her closely, gauging every twitch of her expression, every breath. "You are now a Ghost. Like us."

She shook her head in slow disbelief. "No. No, they wouldn't—Locke wouldn't—" She swallowed, her hands tightening into fists.

"Can you play the newscast for us, Clarence?" I asked

The screen went blank then a title bar scrolled across.

BROADCAST VIA THE TRUTH NETWORK

...followed by scrolling text and a voice over:

"It is with great sorrow that we report the loss of one of New Columbia's finest. Captain Evelyn Rayne, a warrior for order and justice, has fallen in the line of duty—sacrificed by the very insurgents who seek to tear down everything we have built."

"Rayne was more than an enforcer—she was a guardian of stability, a protector of the system that keeps us strong. She stood against the chaos of the Undercity, against the corruption of those who would undermine our perfect society. And in doing so, she paid the ultimate price."

"The so-called 'Ghost Network'—these cowards lurking beneath our feet—knew that she was close to exposing them. They feared her. They feared what she knew. And so, rather than face justice, they did what rebels always do. They silenced her."

"The enemies of New Columbia have revealed themselves, and they will not go unanswered. We will not mourn Evelyn Rayne with tears—we will honor her with action. We will bring her killers to justice. We will root out this infection. And we will ensure that her sacrifice was not in vain. Every one of the Ghosts SHALL BE TERMINATED."

TRANSMISSION END

I stepped closer, lowering my head, "Every one of the Ghosts shall be terminated" I said, "and you are a ghost". Then I echoed her earlier words.

"Hope you don't mind some visitors."

Evelyn's hands clenched into fists. I thought she might strike me. I watched as the realization hit her. Locke had thrown her to the wolves. She had been loyal. She had risked everything to protect the Algorithm, the city, the system that had raised her— And now it had cast her out. Just like it had cast out all of us. She said nothing more after the broadcast ended. She stood, motionless, staring at nothing.

I was painfully aware that she had just lost more than any of us. We had chosen this fight. She'd been betrayed and erased from it.

I took a breath. "So…Evelyn, what now?"

Adam didn't answer. No one did.

That was when Evelyn spoke. Quietly. Firmly.

"We leave."

We all turned to her. She met my gaze, then Adam's.

"You showed me yourselves. Somewhere out there," she said, pointing toward the walls of New Columbia, "there's another world. Not this... this...." She gestured to the screens flashing Callus' propaganda. "...whatever this is."

Adam frowned. "We don't know what's out there."

Evelyn's jaw tightened. "We know what's in here!"

That was the truth of it, wasn't it? We couldn't stay here. Up until Clarence had found the file, we hadn't even considered the possibility that there was an outside world. The Algorithm had made sure of that. For as long as we'd lived, we had been told that New Columbia was all that was left. That the world beyond the walls had collapsed into chaos. That Callus had saved us. And yet, the External Media files told a different story. A world thriving without us. A world that had cut New Columbia off like a diseased limb. A world we could reach—if we could get out.

I looked around the room. We were a handful of Ghosts. Erased from society, and now facing an onslaught of Enforcers bearing down to destroy what was left of us. After a moment I asked what I believe we were all wondering.

"Mind if we come with you?"

Adam exhaled sharply, but there was no argument in his expression. He was already considering the possibilities. The risks. The reality that staying was no longer an option.

Clarence scoffed. "OK, Hang on. Let's say we try. How do we leave? The walls are covered with turrets, the city is locked down, and we don't even know what's on the other side. The drones will be watching the walls."

Lee had stood by quietly up until now, arms crossed, brows furrowed as they considered the problem. Then, slowly, they lifted their head.

"You're all thinking like city dwellers," they said. "Looking up. Looking out."

They took a step forward, locking eyes with each of us.

"Stop looking up. Go under!"

Adam squinted. "Under what?"

"The city. The walls. The whole damn system," Lee shrugged. "Y'all keep looking for an exit up top—over fences, through checkpoints. But I've been slipping through cracks in this city my whole life."

Clarence leaned forward. "You're saying there's a way out underground?"

Lee gave him a pointed look.

"I used to hide from people up there," they said, voice casual—but I caught the edge beneath it.

Lee had never talked much about life before they were offloaded. But they didn't have to. I'd seen it before—people like Lee weren't just discarded because their SES score dropped too low. They were pushed. Nudged out. A thousand little slights. A thousand invisible hands, pressing down, telling them they didn't belong. The SES stood for Socio-Economic Standing, and people like Lee found themselves automatically handicapped on the low end of the 'socio-' score, with little hope of balancing it out on the 'economic' side. They were pretty much destined to be offloaded. Too many people thought that that fact alone made it OK to bully them.

"I spent a lot of time in the tunnels back then," Lee continued. "Hiding where the little assholes were too afraid to follow. Deep in the tunnels. That's where I found it."

I frowned. "What?"

"There's a place—deeper than anything mapped. A tunnel that predates all of this."

Clarence's brow furrowed. "Predates what?"

Lee hesitated, then said, "New Columbia."

I swallowed. "You think it leads outside?"

Lee gave one of their famous goofy grins. "Only one way to find out."

Adam glanced back at the monitors, watching the Enforces thrash the markets. Then he turned to us, eyes dark.

"We don't have time. We move." No one argued.

Evelyn looked at the monitor that showed the Enforcers crashing through the crowds. Then she looked over to the screen showing the people chanting for Callus' to restore control. A lifetime of defending Callus and his Oligarchs, blind loyalty to the system and its perfect order. And now there it was, flayed open to expose the rotten carnage beneath. And yet they still wanted Callas to stave them

She slowly shook her head. "I guess you can't fix stupid."

Adam let out a long breath. Then, slowly, he nodded. One by one, the others did too. We weren't going to save New Columbia. Now it was time to save ourselves.

Lee led us deep into the Undercity, through passageways even the Ghosts didn't use.

The tunnels were narrow, damp, filled with the scent of mildew and stagnant water. Old industrial pipelines ran along the walls, rusted and forgotten.

I had to duck beneath low-hanging beams, squeezing between collapsed debris and twisted metal. Evelyn grunted as she hauled herself through a particularly tight gap.

"How the hell did you ever get this far down here in the first place?" she muttered.

"I got really good at running," Lee said simply. "I also thought this place was pretty cool. Still do."

We walked for hours. No maps. No markers. Just Lee, leading us through a maze of old transit corridors and collapsed infrastructure. Then they stopped and held their hands against the wall like a game-show personality showcasing a prize. Behind Lees hands, an ancient, rusted sign, half-buried in grime and decay.

BRICKEY'S LANDING – BORDER CROSSING.

On the other wall was another sign, pock marked and nearly undecipherable. I rubbed at the dirt, and stopped, seeing I was knocking the paint of. I blew off some of the dust and barely made out the letters.

CHECKPOINT
NOW LEAVING NEW COLUMBIA

Adam let out a low whistle.

"Well, I'll be damned."

"OK" I said, pointing. "So... How do we get through that?"

The tunnel ended at a solid wall of concrete. No gate. No gaps. No way through. Defeat settled in. I dropped onto a pile of debris, head in my hands. Clarence was nearby, exploring the sides of the tunnel, poking through the debris. He paused, squinting at something. Then—

"Maybe here?"

He pulled at a large piece of sheet metal that had

been pinned against the wall by fallen concrete and re-bar. —and the metal shifted a little. Lee and I joined, then Adam as we cleared the piles of rock and rubble enough to free the heavy scrap. Together, we heaved the piece backwards letting it fall to the ground. A cloud of dust and grit enveloped us, blinding us a moment before we could see what lay behind it, hidden from sight.

A door. It was locked of course, but not impenetrable. Excited, the team went to work. Adam found a steel beam and the five of us used it as a ram rod. The noise of the metal on metal was deafening. But we were deep into the abyss - we weren't worried about being heard. After three good hits, the old, rusted metal began to give way.

Adam paused, holding his hand up.

"One more time, on the count of three."

And then—with a final violent strike — It swung open. The first thing I noticed was the air. Cool. Fresh. No metallic tang. No artificial sterility. We stepped through, one by one, into the open world beyond the walls. A bridge stretched before us, crossing a wide, slow-moving river. Beyond it— Not wasteland. Not desolation. Fields. Trees. A sky not choked in industrial haze.

And then—we saw the van. White. Electric. A green cross printed on the side. It stopped just beyond the bridge.

The driver stepped out, shielding her eyes with one hand, watching us cross over the river. As we drew near, I saw the words printed in small green lettering under the green cross symbol.

IMMIGRANT SERVICES - OFFICIAL USE ONLY

When we were finally within earshot she waved and walked towards us.

"Welcome," she said. "Let's get you out of those clothes and get some warm food into you. You look like you've been through hell."

END OF BOOK 1

Epilogue

I woke to the sound of water. A soft trickle, the hush of leaves shifting in the breeze. For a moment, I forgot where I was. The bed beneath me wasn't hard, wasn't cold. The air smelled of flowers, green and alive. Sunlight streamed through a lattice of vines overhead, casting shifting patterns across the silk sheets. A garden.

Not metal. Not concrete. Not the buzz of city drones or the static haze of digital surveillance. I sat up slowly. Through the open balcony doors, the skyline stretched in soft curves and glass towers, nothing like the brutal angles of New Columbia. In the distance, I saw the shimmer of a river—wide, slow-moving, untouched by waste or industry. It was beautiful.

And I didn't trust it for a second.

A voice pulled me from my thoughts. "You're up." I turned to see Adam standing near the window, his hands in his pockets, his reflection a faint blur in the glass. He looked…different here. Lighter. Or maybe just untethered. The weight of survival had defined him for so long, and now, for the first time, he wasn't running. But that didn't mean he was staying.

"What's the verdict?" I asked.

Adam exhaled, shaking his head. "It's everything they promised. No poverty. No crime. No currency. No one struggling to meet quotas or claw their way up a ranking system." He glanced at me. "No SES."

I leaned back against the pillows. "Sounds like a dream."

His jaw tightened. "It's a dream because they had the luxury to make it one. We didn't. We let New Columbia happen."

I felt that truth settle between us. We could have stopped it. Could have intervened. Instead, New Columbians had watched from their positions of safety and security, letting millions suffer inside a prison of their own making. Letting the Offloaded disappear. I swung my legs out of bed, the cool tile grounding me.

"It's not finished, is it? We have to go back."

Adam did not argue. He never would. He was already thinking about it. Planning. Our thoughts were broken by a second voice.

"I played the part of Marla," Evelyn's voice cut in from the doorway. "The woman obsessed with revenge. The woman who would do anything to take down the man who betrayed her."

She stepped forward, her blue-gray eyes sharp, edged with something new. Something dangerous. She crossed her arms.

"I think I'd like to play that role for real."

I studied her. Evelyn Rayne, the enforcer. The weapon of the ISB. The most feared hunter in the city. Now erased. Now a ghost. Her target? It was not hard to guess. Locke.

Adam met my gaze. I nodded. We were going back. But this time, we were not running.

This time, we would be the ones hunting.

AUTHOR'S NOTE

The concept of Singularity, the point at which AI surpasses human intelligence and evolves beyond our control, is no longer just a theory. Whether it happens in the next six months or the next ten years, its arrival is inevitable. And when it does come, it will not be a single moment of change, but a cascade of advancements that will alter our reality in ways we cannot yet comprehend.

The sheer computational power of an intelligence beyond human limitation will enable things that seem impossible today—instant medical cures, limitless energy, an end to scarcity itself. Within it lies the chance to usher in an era of prosperity and equity unlike anything in history.

The choice of whether AI becomes our salvation or our downfall does not belong to the machines. It belongs to us. To the policies we enact, the values we instill, and the vigilance we uphold against those who would use it to serve power instead of people. In the end, technology will not determine our fate. We will.

And as long as we fight for transparency, accountability, and the fundamental dignity of every human being, then no system—no Algorithm—will ever truly own us.

Thank you for taking this journey with me.

— S. Stuart Richardson, March, 2025